Also by RM Atkins

Pools of Unheard Tears

Revenge on High

London Under Threat

COUNTDOWN

BY

RM ATKINS

1

"Bloody hell, the temperature must have dropped overnight. I'm freezing!" said Bill as he reached out for the duvet; his normally very snug duvet though was nowhere within his reach. Bill realised that the only explanation for his absent cover was the fact that it had fallen off his bed and was at this moment in time, keeping the carpet warm instead of him. After groping, all around him with his eyes still tightly closed, without any success. Bill decided to force his tired eyes to open and actually go and look for the missing cover. As his eyes began to open, he was surprised that a bright light was shining into them.

"Oh shit, don't tell me I didn't turn off the light when I went to bed again," said Bill as he swung his legs to the side to get out of bed.

"What the hell's going on?"

Instead of Bill's feet dropping down from his bed onto his bedroom carpet, for some reason they stayed level. After pushing himself up to lean back onto his elbows, Bill tried to work out what was going on. As his eyes began to change from a blurred outlook to finally coming into focus, his only added to Bill's confusion. He found that he was not in his bedroom at home but was for some reason lying on grass out in the open!

"What the fuck's going on here?" said Bill aloud. "And where the hell am I?"

Bill turned his head around nervously from side to side but all that he could see was a view of a very rugged landscape. This consisted of hills and rocky outcrops with grassy slopes, leading down the hillside and out of sight!

"Christ is this some sort of bad dream I'm having?" thought Bill to himself. "Well if it is then it is very realistic, in every way!"

Bill tried to stand up so that he could get a better look around him. Unfortunately, as he tried to stand, he discovered that his legs for some unknown reason could not hold his weight.

"What's happening to me?" thought Bill as he dropped back down onto the hard ground.

It was the beginning of November, and the air temperature was turning very cold. It was at least an hour before Bill's legs were working properly, and he was able to stand up for a better look around. The scenery was very imposing, yet stunning.

Throughout the 360-degree turn from where he was standing. Bill could only see a very rugged countryside that was totally devoid of any other signs of life. Bill then started to shake with the cold and instinctively began to rub his hands up and down on his arms and legs to try to get the circulation working. It was only then that he noticed that he was only wearing a white t-shirt and a pair of boxer shorts. He looked around for any sign of his missing clothes but there were none.

"I don't understand what has happened to me?" said Bill to himself. "The last thing that I remember is going out for a drink in one of the bars close to where I live. How the hell I've ended up here, is beyond me."

It was then, that another thought entered Bill's head and this one was very frightening. If he was here, then where were his wife and son?

Bill stood up and looked once again all around him this time tough with more fervour. "Roz, Sammy, where are you?" screamed Bill at the top of his voice, at the same time running from side to side hoping to catch sight of them!

Time after time, Bill cupped his hands around his mouth and shouted out their names in every direction, but to no avail. From his high point, there was no sign of either member of his family. Despair quickly shrouded Bill at the thought of his wife and son alone somewhere like this and he was not there to look after them. The cold ground striking up and into his body was what finally shook Bill out of his doldrums. That was when his thoughts turned to being more positive and trying to find a way out of this God forsaken place and to go look for them.

Bill began to jog on the spot hoping to generate some warmth in his now cold body. It was then that he caught his right foot on a sharp piece of stone that had been sticking out of the ground. Immediately, he let out a loud scream of agony and he reached down and grabbed a hold of his injured foot. At first, Bill was afraid to look closely at it in case it had been cut and was now bleeding. Then, slowly he released the tight hold that he had around his foot allowing him to examine the injury more closely. To his delight, Bill found that apart from it being sore there was no other injury that was visible to his foot.

"I have no idea what has happened to me," thought Bill. "But whatever I do next, I mustn't damage my feet anymore. They are my only means for me to try to escape from this place, wherever this place is. Well at least after that amount of pain from my foot, I'm now convinced that I am not dreaming all of this. Unless, that is, it's some sort of horrible nightmare?"

Sitting back down on the ground, Bill took off his t-shirt and proceeded to tear it up into strips. He had to ensure that they were large enough for him to wrap around his feet for protection from the sharp rocks. It took a little while to achieve this but soon he was able to stand up and feel more confident walking about.

Bill then had a good look around him hoping to see some type of shack or building that might have smoke rising up to tell him that there was help close by. Unfortunately, he could not see any signs that would indicate as to which direction he should take to assist with his rescue.

Bill looked for the easiest route down the hillside from where he was and then edged his way down. After about an hour of walking, he found himself standing in a small valley that stood between two tall rocky hillsides. Looking down the slope that was in front of him, Bill could see that the entire path ahead of him was covered in sharp pieces of stone and rock.

"If I try to get down there, I will rip my feet to shreds," thought Bill as he looked around him. To his dismay, he realised that apart from the way that he had just come from, all of the other possible routes were going to be too difficult to attempt especially without any type of proper footwear. So, with a heavy heart, Bill took the only option left to him and turned around and made his way back to where he had started from. Although the journey to the rocky outcrop only took him an hour to reach, the climb back up the slope took almost double.

Although the wind was icy cold, the climb back up the steep slope had taken its toll on Bill. For now, not only was his extremities cold to the touch, the effort that had been needed to climb back up to where he had started from had made him sweat profusely. Now there were areas of his body now covered with perspiration moisture that was beginning to freeze. Shelter out of this deadly wind was going to be essential if he was going to survive this ordeal.

Standing back where he had begun Bill looked for some sort of inspiration as to which direction he should take next!

"Why is it, only the people that hardly ever go into the countryside are the ones that usually end up getting lost?" thought Bill as he rescanned the horizon.

Then he heard a sound that was being brought to him on the passing wind. Bill turned his head so that he could hear what the sound was more clearly. It took a little while before Bill managed to pick out he thought were dogs barking. As he listened to discover from which direction the sound was coming from. The barking sounds appeared to be getting louder and closer to where he was standing.

"Could this be a Hunt passing close to me?" thought Bill scanning the entire area looking for the hunting pack of hounds.

At first where the sounds were coming from were hard to pin point due to the strong wind. Then as he strained his ears to hear more clearly, the barking sounds altered to a very distinct howl. The first howl that he had heard was then followed by several other howls. This eerie echoing sound made Bill's heart skip a beat at the thought of what type of animal was making that noise. He looked towards the direction of the sound for any indication as to what was heading his way.

Then in the distance, Bill could just make out the shapes of dog like animals running in what looked like a pack formation. A deep painful ache came into the pit of his stomach and his feet seemed to be frozen to the spot looking at the snarling animals that appeared to be heading at a very fast pace towards him. Bill dropped onto the ground and crawled on his stomach up to the crest of the hill. Then while keeping his head down close to the ground, he slowly peeped through the short grass down into the valley below. There he could see quite clearly, a pack of dogs that were all circling about snapping and snarling as they sniffed the air.

"Oh shit, if I'm not mistaken, those look very much like a pack of wolves and they look very hungry. I bet that they are trying find where I am, my sweaty scent that must be travelling to them on the wind," thought Bill as he watched the pack moving about. "But I don't understand where in England are there packs of wild wolves roaming the countryside?"

Then for some unknown reason, Bill licked the end of his index finger and held it close to the top of the hillside. Within seconds, he could feel the cold breeze blowing onto his wet finger from in front of him.

"Ah, the wind is blowing towards me, meaning that I am up wind and that is why the pack cannot find my scent. Well that is what they always say on those wildlife programmes that you see on the TV," said Bill half smiling to himself. "Bloody hell, this must be the first thing that I've done right since waking up this morning!"

Bill then heard howling coming from down where the pack were and he decided to have another peep. There he saw one of the largest wolves sitting on a raised mound in front of the pack, with his huge head held back and howling up into the air. That sound made every hair on Bill's body stand on end as he watched events unfold below him. When, what Bill believed was the pack leader finished howling, he turned and began heading off down the hillside taking the rest of the baying pack with him. Bill could not bring himself to move until the pack had totally disappeared from his sight.

Then as he made a final look around, something further on down the other side of the slope caught his eye. It looked as though it might be a small cave or at least an overhang where he might be able to get some shelter from the icy wind. It wasn't until he had stood up off the ground, did he realise just how cold the ground had actually been. In fact, the moisture that had been transferred from his body where he'd laid on the ground now appeared to be turning white as he looked at it. Bill believed that it could easily turn to being a frost if the air temperature was to drop much further.

He decided to chance it and headed off at a fast pace down the hillside towards it. seemed that he had been running fast for ages, occasionally tripping over stones along the way. All the time there was the distant sound of these dogs that were for some reason hunting him down. Soon he was within striking distance of what looked like a small cave and that was set back into the rocky overhang. The thought of getting out of the icy wind and out of sight of those animals encouraged Bill to quickly clamber up the side of the rough hill. It was when he was within a few metres of the opening to the cave; Bill stopped and stared up at the cave.

"I wonder if there are any other wild animals living in there?" thought Bill feeling hesitant to move closer. "But hang on a minute, there are no wild animals in this country, are there. But what about the wolves that had been after me?" he thought to himself.

He felt that he was now in a quandary, does he enter the cave and get out of this icy wind and hopefully escape from that pack of wolves that are chasing him. Or, does he try to discover if there is anything else living in there.

"Oh this is bloody stupid!" said Bill aloud.

"Or am I going to be that unlucky to run into two lots of animals that want me on their dinner menu?"

Bill pushed those thoughts to the back of his mind and began to quickly climb further on up the slope then, a sudden thought entered his head.

"Hang on a minute though. How do I know what country I am actually in right now? First I go out for a drink in London and then I wake up virtually naked on the top of a barren hillside in God only knows where. All this is too bizarre for me, fuck it I'm freezing my nuts off out here, so I'm going inside the cave and to hell with the consequences!"

At the entrance to the cave, Bill stopped briefly and with his heart thumping in his throat called out to see if there was any reply. It was a heart stopping moment as he waited for the echoed call into the cave to cease and then the wait for some type of a response to emanate back to him. After a few seconds of complete silence, Bill convinced himself that it was safe for him to enter the cave. Using the light from the entrance, he edged his way into the cave, and found a place behind some rocky ledges out of the wind and sat down for a rest. Feeling a little warmer being for the first time since waking out of the icy wind, Bill began to relax and tried to make some sense of his crazy predicament.

He looked around at the walls of the cave for any signs, as to where in the world he actually was at this moment in time. The air inside the cave smelt damp and the walls were icy to the touch. He turned and looked back over his shoulder at the view from the entrance to the cave.

"Where in the world could this place be?" thought Bill now feeling slightly warmer now that he was out of the icy wind. "Shit, for all I know I could be on Dartmoor, or on a remote hillside in Wales or Scotland. It's strange that there are no features at all for me to get any sort of bearing as to where the hell I am. If I am still in one of those places, do they have any wolf packs roaming about that are wild? Christ, I'm not a country boy; I've lived all of my life in the big cities. Talk about being a duck out of water!"

For the moment, he gave up trying to find the answer to that question, as an icy blast of wind made its way inside the cave. Bill slumped down so that he was leaning with his head and shoulders against a large boulder. The ground that was beneath him was almost a sandy texture and seemed to help him to generate some trifles of heat into his cold body.

Then he remembered those wolves that had been after him and he focused his ears to listen for them. For a couple of minutes, Bill hardly took a breath as he listened intently for any type of sound. After five minutes or so, Bill relaxed when the sound of the baying pack, still could not be heard.

It was while his mind was spinning round trying to work out what had happened to him, a strong smell emanated deep into his nostrils. At first, he thought that it was the smell of the cave from the moisture in the walls and the ground, then, he wasn't so sure. Standing up, Bill sniffed the air and decided to follow the strong smell. Moving slowly, as the light reduced as he moved further into the cave, Bill looked before placing every step. Then in the corner on the floor, Bill could just make out a lump lying on the floor of the cave.

"What is it?" thought Bill, not really knowing if he should move closer or not!

Then fumbling on the floor, Bill managed to find a couple of small stones and picked them up. He then aimed at the mound on the floor and threw the two stones at the same time. As the stones made their way towards the mound, Bill was ready to make a quick retreat if the mound turned out to be a danger to him. The two stones hit their target with no reaction. This gave Bill a bit more confidence to approach and find out what it is. Step by cautious step, Bill moved a little closer. Soon he was within reach of touching whatever was there. Bill nervously stretched out his shaking hand towards the mound and touched it. Immediately he made contact, Bill quickly withdrew his hand. When nothing happened, Bill moved a little closer and placed his hand back onto the mound and this time he took the time to actually feel what was there. To his astonishment, what he was touching was the fleece of a dead sheep. As he tried to move it, the strong smell of rotting flesh almost burnt into his throat.

Bill dragged the fleece to the entrance of the cave for a closer look. In the daylight, he could see that the majority of the animal's flesh had completely decayed, leaving only the bony carcass of the sheep behind. That was when he noticed that the rapid shaking of the sheep's fleece, had resulted in it tearing along its underbelly, allowing it to be opened up like a dirty old coat!

He dragged the fleece with the sheep's remains out of the cave and proceeded to shake to contents out. He made sure that he was standing up wind from the rotting pieces of flesh. Especially when they were all being strewn about in the air as he quickly flicked the sheep's fleece up and down to get rid of any unwanted body parts.

Bill was by the end of this totally exhausted and with the fleece in hand he went back into the cave out of the wind and sat down leaning against the rock with the fur side of the fleece now covering his bare body. That was when his ears suddenly heard the sounds of dogs howling once more. It was then that Bill realised what a stupid mistake he had just made. In throwing the rotting remains of that sheep outside the cave, the smell had obviously attracted the hungry pack of wolves up to where he now was hiding.

In a panic, Bill snatched up the fleece and headed further into the cave looking for somewhere to hide that was both safe and out of sight. Frantically he scoured the darkened area for a safe hiding place but there was none to be found!

Then with the sound of the wolves near to the entrance of the cave, fighting over the decaying remains. Bill's eyes spotted through the shadows a small ledge part way up the side of the cave wall. So with fleece in hand, Bill began the steep climb up the side wall of the cave. Soon his right hand felt the ledge above him and he managed to throw the fleece up onto it. Now with two free hands, Bill was able to climb that bit easier. He was just about to pull himself up onto the ledge and safety when he felt an agonising pain generate up through his left leg. Bill let out a loud scream as the extreme pain generated up through his leg. Though the pain was agonising, Bill had to concentrate hard on keeping his grip on the small ledge so that he did not fall back down onto the ground into the middle of the snarling wolves. As the intense pain increased, Bill took a second to glance down under his arms to see what was the cause of such pain and was immediately confronted by two reddish dead coloured eyes staring back up at him. There was what looked like a large wolf like animal hanging onto his left foot with its sharp teeth wrapped tightly around Bill's foot. It was trying, using all of his body weight to make Bill lose his grip and fall back into the middle of the hunting pack. As his head flicked from side to side, tearing at Bill's foot. Great globules of white saliva sprayed out from the sides of his mouth.

Instinctively, Bill kicked out with his right foot at the wolf's face and hit it hard on the end of its snout. This action made it yelp out in pain and then letting go of the bite hold that it had on his foot. As the animal fell back down hard onto the ground below, Bill managed to drag himself up onto the ledge and into comparative safety. Below him, Bill could see the pack of dogs circling round and looking up to where he was. Time after time, one of the dogs would try to run and scramble up the sidewall of the cave to get at him. Each time thankfully they failed. Bill had to try to position his body so that it was out of reach to the wolves' sharp teeth, but was ready and able to kick out to defend himself if one of the animals got too close to him.

After what seemed an age, the wolves gave up on their attempts to scale the cave walls after Bill. Instead, they fixed their minds and teeth onto a pile of old sheep's bones that they had dragged into the cave from outside. Bill soon received a stark reminder of what would happen to him if he were to somehow slip off the small ledge and fall into their ravenous grasp. As he lay back on the rough stony ledge, trying to get some rest. The constant sound of bones being broken and crushed in powerful jaws, echoed deep into the cave.

After about an hour of commotion, the pack began to settle down and eventually they all lay down and fell quiet. Through the half-light, Bill would occasionally see one of their eyes open and look up to where he was just to make sure that he was still there.

Bill eventually began to relax knowing that they could not reach him. He used some of the torn up t-shirt to bind the wounds on his foot and to stem the bleeding. Then feeling totally exhausted, Bill lay back and pulled the fleece over him. Within minutes, he could feel the warmth generating through him from the sheep's fleece and he drifted off into a deep sleep.

He began to think of his friends and family and wondered if he would ever see them again, or would this surreal place be where his life will prematurely come to an end?

———————

2

At ten o`clock on a late November night, Dave Geraint was sitting watching television. This was the first Saturday night back after spending a week's holiday with some friends down in Cornwall. Since his promotion to Detective Chief Inspector along with his friend and work colleague's promotion to Inspector Bill Spears. This holiday had been the first that Dave had taken for over twelve months. His time spent with friends in Cornwall had been very relaxing in contrast to the busy hubbub of London. Now back, Dave felt refreshed and was looking forward to going back to work at New Scotland Yard on Monday, where he was attached to the Serious Crime Squad.

So with a large bowl of popcorn and a couple of cans of beer sitting on the table next to him,

Dave was now all set to watch a film on his telly. Just as his program was about to begin, there came a loud banging on his front door!

"Who the bloody hell is that, this time of night!" cursed Dave as he stood up and went to the front window to have a look outside. With the light of and only the light showing from his TV, Dave moved the curtain to one side to see who was banging on his door like that. Immediately that he moved the curtain, he saw blue flashing lights to the left and to the right of his front gate. Craning his neck to peep towards the front door, he could just make out the uniform of a police officer standing there.

"What's going on?" said Dave aloud to himself.

Dave moved from the window to the front door and cautiously opened it. "What is going on?" asked Dave to the WPC who was standing there.

"I'm sorry sir but I have no time to tell you right now!" replied the WPC in an official tone of voice. "There is a suspect device in that car that is parked outside your front gate, and I have to evacuate everyone that is close proximity for their own safety." As she took hold of Dave's arm and virtually pulled him out of his doorway and onto the garden front path.

"But?" replied Dave

"Look sir, this is for your own safety, please will you come with me now!" said the WPC moving Dave to one side and pulling his front door to with a slam.

Dave, watched in disbelief, and shrugged his shoulders and proceeded to follow the WPC. They then clambered over next doors front garden fence then down his path and through his front gate. Dave was then ushered to a holding point where he met up with some of his other neighbours.

"Hello Dave," said Phil, his next-door neighbour. "Have you got any idea what the hell's going on here?"

"Sorry, I only came back from holiday today and was just settling down to watch a film when I heard someone banging on my front door. The rest you already know seeing that you are here too," said Dave, wishing that he had managed to grab hold of a coat before being frogmarched out of his house.

Just then, the WPC walked close by and Phil decided to go and ask her what was happening out there. "Excuse me officer," said Phil politely. "Can you tell us what is going on and how long it will be before we can all return to our homes again?"

The WPC stopped in her tracks and stood there with her hands akimbo and replied, "Look sir, you will all have to wait along with the other people until we are told that you can safely return to your homes!" replied the WPC, in a very official tone of voice.

"Look, all I was asking is why we have all been ejected out of our homes at this time of night, standing around in the cold without any explanation?" replied Phil sounding a little miffed at her response to his question.

The WPC though did not reply to Phil's question and began to walk off. "Do you think that you could find out what is going on for us Dave?" asked Phil with exasperation in his voice. However, before Dave could reply the WPC who must have heard Phil ask Dave, did an about turn on her heels and came back.

"Look I have explained to you more than once, that you will be told as soon as it is safely possible to return to your home. So I do not think that asking anyone else to intervene will have any effect on that matter, do you sir?" replied the WPC obviously getting agitated at Phil's questions.

"Excuse me officer," said Dave in a calm voice. "Why won't you explain to these people your reasoning behind not telling them what the problem is?"

With that the WPC must have reached her limit and turned away from Dave and began to walk off, much to the disgust of the people that were left standing about.

"Officer! I would like to have a quiet word with you," said Dave as he moved slightly away from the others.

"Look sir, I can't stand here all night discussing what you should or should not be told. Have I made myself clear!" replied the WPC.

"Oh you have made yourself very clear indeed," said Dave in a much louder voice. "Now I would like you to either tell me who is actually in charge here, or you can go and fetch that officer for me, right now!"

The WPC now realising that she was getting nowhere with this person and after looking directly back at Dave and giving off a deep sigh, she walked off. A few seconds later, she, returned along with another police officer. "What appears to be the problem here?" said the police officer sounding very irritable that he had been disturbed.

"Are you the person who is in charge of this operation?" asked Dave politely.

"No, he is too busy to be coming in here to answer questions all of the time," replied the officer.

"Oh, well do you think that you could possibly give him a message from me then?" said Dave calmly.

"If I get time," replied the officer sharply and only half listening, to what was being said to him. "Well what is it?"

"Would you tell him that Detective Chief Inspector Geraint of New Scotland Yard would like a few seconds of his time please!" replied Dave, as he turned away from them and then returned to the group of his neighbours. His actions were greeted with a few cheers and a ripple of applause. To which Dave just smiled back to them and bowed his head as a sarcastic thank you.

As the other looked on, the look on both the WPC and the other officer's face was priceless, as they quickly realised the big bollock that they had both dropped in front of a very senior police officer and his friends.

The two PCs appeared not to know what to do next and just both stood there almost transfixed at their unenviable situation. The from out of the shadows, yet another police officer arrived on the scene.

"Hello everyone, I am Inspector Brown and I am pleased to be able to inform you that everything is now safe for you all to return back to your own home."

This news from the inspector was received with a mixed reception, especially seeing as the people had all been ousted out of their homes into a cold night without any information as to the reasons why! On the one hand, they were all glad to be getting back indoors but on the other, they were upset at the way they'd all been treated! It was as Inspector Brown was turning to leave, he noticed a familiar face in the crowd.

"Hello sir, what are you doing here?" said the inspector to Dave.

"Oh hello," replied Dave when he recognised who it was talking to him. "Well like the rest of the people here I was virtually dragged out of my house over there by, shall we say, a very officious WPC and brought over here and then left with these other people. At least she did tell me that there was a potential bomb in a car parked outside my place. So I suppose that, I at least knew more than the others did!"

"Yes and she was very rude to us when we asked what was going on!" spouted out one of the people that were still standing around.

Inspector Brown now seemed at a loss for words. He had gone from coming to deliver some, what he thought was good news to the people that were waiting to return home.

Instead, he finds himself in the unexpected role of being a mediator.

"Well I'm very sorry to hear about your unacceptable experience during this tricky situation. Can I ask you to leave it with me to investigate your concerns regarding your treatment tomorrow?" said Inspector Brown to the people that were still there.

Amid some grumbling the consensus of opinion from them all, was to let him get on with it so that they could all get back indoors and into the warm again. Soon the only people that remained were the two PCs, Inspector Brown and Dave.

"You handled that very well Peter. It is Peter isn't it?" said Dave.

"Thank you sir, yes it is Peter, and I'm sorry about the inappropriate impression that these two have made while this caper was going on!"

"Tell me are these two still probationers?" asked Dave looking directly at the two PCs who sheepishly hung their heads down and said nothing in reply to Dave's question.

"Yes I think so," replied Peter glaring at them.

"Well may I suggest that they both do a refresher course on how to deal with the members of the public in future!" said Dave turning away from them.

"That is already noted," replied Peter. "Now it might be time for us to leave and for you to return to your home."

"Ah, that could be a bit of a problem?" said Dave looking directly at the WPC. "You see, when I was escorted out of my house by this WPC. She slammed the front door to before I was able to collect my door keys from out of my coat pocket. So now, I have no way of getting back into my house. Now that problem is I believe going to be up to you Inspector Brown, to sort that out for me. Wouldn't you say?"

"Oh for Christ sake you didn't do that did you?" said Peter to the WPC with a sound of total exasperation in his voice.

"But how was I to know that he was a DCI, when I knocked on his door?" said the WPC trying hard to justify her actions.

"That was the whole problem from the start," replied the Inspector. "It shouldn't have made any difference whether it was a DCI or an old lady. It was your duty to make sure that they were all escorted away from any danger but at the same time ensure that they had keys so that they could return home later. Therefore, I think that the both of you should go across to DCI Geraint's home and get that front door open without causing any damage. Do I make myself clear?"

"Yes sir," they both replied in unison.

"But how do we gain access to the DCI's home without forcing his front door?" asked the WPC sounding a little confused.

"That will be down to your skills and ingenuity as police officers," replied Inspector Brown with a glare in his eyes and indicating with his hand to move off quickly and get on with it! "I'm sorry about this sir," said Peter apologetically to Dave.

"That's alright, they had to learn this lesson at some time," replied Dave smiling. "I just wish that it hadn't been on my last day's holiday, that's all!"

It was about forty-five minutes later, when Dave finally managed to gain access to his home. The officers managed to get a hold of a locksmith who came out and opened his front door for him. Where the bill for doing the job was sent to though, is still unknown!

3

"Has anyone seen Bill this morning?" asked Dave as he entered the office.

Dave Geraint is now a Detective Chief Inspector in the Serious Crime Department at new Scotland Yard in London. After he along with Bill Spears and other members of their specialised team, had all received promotions after saving London from a devastating explosion. Bill, whose official title was now Detective Inspector William Spears, had worked closely with Dave over the past few years and knew that it was unusual for him not to be one of the first to arrive in the office.

The response from the others was a complete negative. It appeared that DI Spears hadn't been seen by anyone that morning. Dave then picked up the phone and tried calling Bill's home number in case he was ill or something like that. Although he tried several times, Dave was unsuccessful in making any contact with him.

His attention was then side-tracked when a note informing him about a shooting that had occurred the previous evening. In the note, it said that a shooting had occurred outside the Lock and Bolt public house on the Eastside of London.

The victim is:

Mr Jamie Peterson aged 40yrs who was married with two children.

"Err, why has this note been put onto my desk?" asked Dave waving the piece of paper about over his head.

"Look, we all know that you've been away on holiday, but surely you recognise the name of the person that had been killed, don't you?" came back the snotty reply.

Dave, hearing this scolding rebuke from someone on the other side of the office, decided to have another look at the victim's name again.

"You're sure of the victim's identity?" called out Dave without raising his head.

"Positive!" came back the reply.

"Oh, shit," replied Dave, taking a deep breath and sitting back in his seat. "This could mean the beginning of a fucking turf war between the East and the West side of London. If the culprit who is responsible for doing this murder is not caught and I mean quickly!"

"Yes we know," came back a reply. "Why do you think that you have been given the job and not one of us?"

Dave lifted his head and looked around to see if he could discover who had just said that remark. Unfortunately, with this new style of office layout, the faces of the other people that worked in his office remained hidden from his view.

"I wish I knew where the hell Bill was this morning," thought Dave as he gathered up the relevant paperwork and made his way out of the office.

Downstairs, DCI Geraint requested a car and driver to take him about on his investigations. About ten minutes later a car drew up alongside him and he quickly sat in the back. The driver was PC Tom Jukes, 25yrs of age and his intentions was to eventually join the elite echelon of high performance police drivers. However, before he could even be considered for a driving trial at such a high level. He would first of all have to prove to the powers to be, that he was a capable driver under normal driving circumstances.

DCI Geraint, once he was seated handed over the address where he wanted to go to the driver. After memorising where he had to go, Tom set off at a fast pace hoping to impress the DCI. However, after only a few minutes into the journey Dave suddenly said, "Tell me driver, have you been entered into a rally or something.

Because it's like sitting on a bucking bronco back here! So unless you know about some urgency that I do not, I want you to slow this bloody car down right now, so that I can get on with some work, alright!"

"Yes sir, sorry sir!" came back the reply from a very sheepish sounding driver.

During the journey across London to the Peterson residence, Dave went over the official reports about where, when and how, the deceased had met his death. Then something that Dave found in the report suddenly struck a chord.

"It says here that Mr Peterson was killed by a shot to the head in St Ives in Cornwall last Friday. If I remember correctly, I was actually there in St Ives on that very day. How bizarre is that?" thought Dave, as he thought back to when he had been there. Yet no matter how hard he tried, he could not remember hearing anything about a shooting taking place.

The police car pulled up outside the address given and the driver opened his window and pressed the intercom button.

"Yes, who's there?" came back a male voice over the speaker.

"This is the police and I have a Detective Chief Inspector Geraint with me and we would like to come in and have a talk with you!" replied the police driver politely.

The intercom crackled and then the electric front gates slowly began to open. As soon as there was enough room, the driver slowly drove the police car through the gates and up to the front door of the property. When the car came to a halt, Dave opened the rear door and got out of the car carrying his folder that had his paperwork inside.

"What do you want me to do while you are inside?" asked the driver.

"Nothing, except for keeping your eyes and ears peeled for anything that seems out of the ordinary," replied the DCI as he walked off towards the front door. "This building is very impressive and must have cost a bundle," thought Dave as he approached the front door.

Dave rang the doorbell and while he waited, took the opportunity to look all around him. The property was old stone built building that looked as though there were numerous bedrooms inside. The gardens were very neat and tidy and seemed to stretch all around the entire house. From time to time, men could be inconspicuously seen moving about at various places around the extremities of the property.

The front door opened and Dave was greeted by two very well built men who were obviously there for the occupant's protection but short on manners.

"Who are you and what do you want here?" asked one of the men.

"As my driver has already informed someone inside. I am DCI Geraint from new Scotland

Yard and I would like to speak to the wife of the deceased man."

"What do you want to see her for?" the other man asked in a rough manner.

"Look, I am here to do my job with regards trying to discover who is responsible for her husband's murder and it doesn't involve speaking to you!" snapped Dave staring directly into the man's face.

Before any response from the two men was made, a female voice was heard from inside telling the two men to show Dave through to her. Immediately the two men parted and stood to one side and gestured with their hands for the DCI to enter. Dave walked behind one of the men along a corridor and he was then showed into a large room.

On entry to the room, Dave was impressed by how opulent the furnishings were and how attractive the woman who was standing in front of him was.

"Hello, I am DCI Geraint from New Scotland Yard."

The female moved towards Dave and held out her hand and replied, "My name is Sonya Peterson and I understand from your conversation just with my late husband, Jamie's colleagues that you are investigating his death."

"That is correct," said Dave with a half-smile.

"Please won't you take a seat," said Sonya.

Dave moved across towards a particular chair that had been indicated to him by the woman, as the place she wanted him to sit down. As soon as he was seated, the door to the room was closed leaving just the two of them alone.

"I must of all apologise for your treatment just now by my late husband's colleagues but they are understandably anxious that I am protected at all costs since the murder of my husband," said Sonya.

"That is only to be expected in the circumstances," replied Dave all the while taking in his surroundings.

"Right then how can I help you with your inquiries?" said Sonya in a composed voice.

"Well, first of all can you tell me what your husband was doing in St Ives?" said Dave watching her every move looking for anything that seemed out of the ordinary.

"From what I am aware, Jamie, had travelled down to St Ives looking for something special for me for a Christmas present," replied Sonya looking down at the carpet.

"Ok, well secondly, can you tell me if he was intending to visit anyone special while he was down there?" asked Dave.

"No, not that I am aware of anyway," said Sonya without any pause.

Dave was just about to ask another question when the door to the room burst open revealing a large well-dressed man, standing there. "What the hell are you doing here?" the man shouted out to Dave.

Dave remained seated but turned slightly to face the obviously angry man who was still standing in the doorway.

"This is DCI Geraint from Scotland Yard Frankie. He has come here to ask some questions so that he can try to find out who it was that killed Jamie," said Sonya, quickly standing up and moving across the room to stand next to the man. "This is Frankie Peterson, Jamie's brother."

Dave stood up and said, "I'm sorry to be here at this trying time but there are certain questions that I must ask if the culprit responsible for this crime is to be caught!"

"Don't you come here with all of your crap statements about how sorry you are? We all know that Jamie's murder just means that there is one less villain for you fucking coppers to worry about!" shouted Frankie out loud.

"Look I understand that you and your family are under a lot of pressure right now. So if it is ok, then I will come back at another time to complete this little chat, Mrs Peterson," said Dave as he walked passed Sonya towards the open doorway. When Dave went to walk passed Frankie his route was blocked, when Frankie moved to stand in front of him. Frankie then leant forward and whispered into Dave ear.

"If you don't know who is responsible for Jamie's death already, then I will tell you. We all know that the Dyer family are responsible for his murder and if you don't arrest one of them, then we will sort this out ourselves!" snapped Frankie standing back up straight.

Dave did not respond to Frankie's statement immediately but after giving his reply, some thought. Dave leant forward and said, "Look you bag of shit for brains, I know that your family run the Eastside of London and the Dyer family do the same over on the Westside. It is common knowledge that between the pair of families, you run prostitution and gambling rackets amongst other things. At this moment in time, they are not my first concern. My unenviable task is to try to discover who is responsible for your brother's murder, so if you have some positive proof of their involvement in this crime then I am ready to hear it. If not, then back off and let me, and my colleagues at the Yard do their job without any interference from you. If not, then you will be seeing a lot more of the police in their official capacity and I don't think for one moment you really want that to happen. Do you!"

Frankie after hearing what Dave had to say, turned and promptly walked away without uttering another word and disappeared into another room.

"I'm sorry about that," said Sonya as she walked with Dave to the front door. "But you must understand that he and the rest of the family are totally devastated by Jamie's murder."

At the front door, Sonya Peterson said her farewells and retired back into the house. Dave climbed back into the car and the police driver made his way down the drive to the front gates. The electric gates were almost open when the police car reached them so they drove straight through without stopping. On the journey back to the Yard, Dave asked the Tom the police driver if he had seen anything that he thought was unusual while he had been waiting.

Tom thought before replying, as he knew that he had managed to piss the DCI off once already today and he didn't want to make it a second.

"Now you that you mention it, there was something. While you were inside the house, I noticed a man standing outside the front gates just staring up the driveway. He just stood there staring, until he was challenged by one of the, rather large men that seemed to be patrolling the grounds. Then he disappeared quickly before they could open the gates and get their hands on him!" said Tom.

"Do you think that you could describe him for me?" asked Dave, trying hard to stay full of wishful thinking.

Tom thought hard then said, "No, he was really too far away for me to get a description, sorry sir!"

"No worries," replied Dave half-smiling. "Oh by the way, well done Tom. It is Tom isn't it, on you noticing that snippet of information anyway!"

"Yes, and thank you for saying so," replied Tom as he turned his complete attention back to his driving so as not to throw the DCI about the car again!

4

Back at the Yard, Dave went straight to his office and once again tried to call through to his old friend Bill Spears. Dave at first tried his home number, in case he had been taken ill and had taken to his bed. There was no response from either his home phone or that of his mobile. He couldn't understand why Bill's wife Rosalynd or little Sammy hadn't answered the phone? Surely, they couldn't all be that ill that no-one could get in touch. Although Dave had this murder case on his desk and he knew that, it was classed as a high priority by the boss's upstairs. Bill's absence was giving Dave an itch that he knew that this itch needed to be scratched!

Dave decided to make the short journey across London to Bill's home to make sure that he was ok. On his way downstairs, Dave made contact with the control room and requested that a car and a driver should be made available to him. Outside the rear of the Yard, the familiar face of his previous police driver, Tom, met DCI Geraint.

Dave handed Bill's address to Tom and asked him to get there a.s.a.p.

Tom said nothing in reply and as soon as the DCI was strapped in, he took off at high speed. On the journey amid the sirens and blue flashing lights, Dave pondered on why Bill had not turned up for work and was not answering any of his phones.

As they were about to enter Bill's road, Dave told Tom to slow down and to turn off both the siren and the flashing blue lights. This he immediately did. Slowly drawing up outside Bill's front gate, Dave took time to have a good look around before he opened the car door and got out.

"Would you like me to come with you sir?" asked Tom eager to get back into the DCI's good books.

"No, I want you to remain here for the moment and observe anything that seems out of the ordinary!" said Dave as he walked towards the front gate.

Tom felt disappointed at the DCI's response but was still eager to try to score some more brownie points before the day was out.

Dave went through the gate and made his way slowly up the path towards the front door. All the time he watched for any movement on the net curtains as he made his approach. After pressing the doorbell, Dave took a half step back from the door for yet another look around. Time and time again, Dave pressed the bell but to no avail.

"Well, Bill is either not there or he is incapacitated in some way," thought Dave shaking his head at the latter thought.

Then under the watchful eyes of his driver Tom, Dave made his way around to the rear of the property. There he repeated his pounding on the backdoor but to no avail. Standing on the step, Dave tried to see if there was any sign of Bill inside but yet again, nothing could be seen. "If this had been anywhere else," thought Dave to himself. "Bill and I would gain entry using whatever means were at our disposal. This though is not anywhere else it's my friend and colleagues home and as yet I have no reason to force an entry or suspect any foul play."

With a heavy heart, Dave returned to the police car then turned back to look at the house one more time. "I know that something isn't right, I can feel it in my bones," said Dave. "But that is not enough for me to force my way into his home without finding something more concrete to work on!"

Dave climbed back into the car and told Tom the driver to take him to the DOG & Duck public house, just around the corner from where they were. Tom could plainly see that the DCI was concerned for his friend, so without replying he drove off towards the pub.

It was only minutes until they arrived at the DOG & DUCK pub and Dave told Tom to stay with the car while he went inside. This was one of Bill's favourite haunts as it wasn't too far for him to walk back home again after having a laugh and a few bevies with his pals. Inside the darkish pub, a casual but reasonably smart man met up with Dave.

"I'm sorry sir, but we are not open yet and I must ask you to leave now!" said the man in a deep tone of voice.

"I am DCI Geraint from the Yard," said Dave taking out his warrant card to show the man. "I am looking for the landlord of this establishment?"

"Oh, that would be me," replied the man holding out his hand to Dave. "My name is Joe Frazer and no I don't mean Frazer the boxer, if you were thinking of that!"

Dave took a hold of Joe's hand and immediately felt the powerful grip tighten around his hand. "No, I wasn't thinking of the boxer but with that strength in your hands I think that maybe I should have!"

"Sorry about that, it's a habit of mine whenever I meet someone new, I like to measure them by their handshake. You though, have surprised me by being able to stand up to the pressure so well!" said Joe smiling.

"Mmm, I am hear looking for one of your patrons that has gone missing and I was wondering if you have seen him lately?" said Dave. "His name is Bill Spears and he is also a good friend of mine."

Joe thought hard for a while then replied, "Is he the plain clothes copper that lives somewhere close to here?"

"Yes, that would be the one," replied Dave eager for some information to start heading his way.

"Well if I remember correctly, he was in here on either Friday or it could have been Saturday night," said Joe still thinking hard.

"Can you remember if he was in here with someone, maybe his wife or another person?" said Dave trying to prompt Joe's memory.

"No he wasn't in here with his misses but I'm pretty sure that he did leave with another bloke though," said Joe.

"Do you think that you could describe this chap for me?" asked Dave taking out his notebook.

"No, sorry, the only thing that I can recall about him was the fact that he was about average height and was aged between forty and sixty," said Joe leaning on the bar as if his mind was completely exhausted from thinking so hard.

Dave made a brief note in his book and thanked Joe for his time, then turned to head for the door. "Oh yes, there was one other thing that might be important," said Joe standing up straight. "The bloke that he left the pub with also had a long full beard. We all thought that he was a little odd because the beard was so untidy it was hard to actually see the face beneath it!"

"Thanks for that," said Dave. "Just one more thing though, can you remember what time they both left here on that night?"

Joe once again worked hard trying to get his brain working so early in the day. "No, sorry, there were just too many people in here for me to be able to remember when any of them left the pub that night or in fact any night!"

"Well it was worth asking just in case you remembered," said Dave as he headed out of the pub and back to the police car.

In the rear of the car, Dave sat quietly going over what Joe had just told him.

"None of this makes any sense!" said Dave aloud.

"Sorry sir," said the driver. "Were you just talking to me?"

"No Tom, I was just recapping on what had been told to me in the pub and none of it makes any sense at all!" said Dave replacing his notebook into his inside pocket.

Dave then took a deep breath and then asked Tom, "Well did anything strange come to your notice, while I was in there chatting?"

"Yes there was something but I'm not sure whether it is relevant or not!" said Tom erring on the side of caution after falling foul of the DCI already once today. "Look, in every case that I have been on, it's the small and sometimes irrelevant sounding things that can turn out to be the crucial turning point.

"Well sir, do you remember when I was waiting for you outside the deceased home earlier on today," said Tom nervously.

"Yes, go on!"

"If you remember that I told you about the man who had been staring up at the house through the gates. Who quickly disappeared when he was approached?"

"Yes, and!"

"Well I'm pretty sure that the very same person was watching this pub while you were inside. It was only when you came out again that I noticed that the man had gone!" said Tom taking a deep breath.

Dave took a few seconds to look out through the side windows of the police car. As he looked up and down the pavements, his mind suddenly began to race. All of the information that he had accumulated from the various people suddenly began buzzing about getting into a complete muddle inside his head.

"Is everything ok sir?" said a voice that brought Dave's mind back into sync so to speak.

Dave sat back and rested his head on the seats headrest while he refocused his thoughts.

"Yes thank, everything is just fine," replied Dave nodding to Tom who was looking at him through the rear mirror. "Oh by the way Tom, were you able to get a better look at this chap this time as before you told me that he had been too far away."

"Yes, a little better that before," said Tom. "I would estimate that he was of average height and was wearing what I would call a full scraggly beard that covered most of his face. In fact, in was that unkempt all you could make out were his eyes."

Dave thought hard about what Tom had just told him and suddenly a thought came into his head and he asked Tom, "Are you positive that the person that you saw was a man and not a woman dressed up to look like a man?"

"Oh shit, oops sorry sir. I never thought that it could have been a woman that was dressing up as a man. I just thought that I was looking at a strange man!" said Tom with a tone of hesitation in his voice.

"Don't you worry about being fooled like that? You will not be the first and definitely will not be the last to be fooled in that way by someone dressing up hoping to fool the police. Remember though that you could be right and it actually was a man that you saw. But you will always remember that feeling that you just had when the other scenario was put to you, won't you!" replied Dave smiling as he remembered when that very same thing had happened to him and Bill once!

"Right Tom, take me back to the Yard will you and this time take the return journey at a more leisurely pace."

5

Back at the Yard, DCI Geraint gathered some of his work colleagues together in the office and gave them instructions. First was for a team to be put on the Dyer family to discover where they go and also to make sure that there are no clashes with the Petersons after the murder. The second was for someone to take Tom the police driver to one side and get him to have a look through some of the snap shots from the villain's gallery in case he could recognise the person that he saw watching them.

The third was to have Tom assigned to him as his driver for the duration of this case, as only he seems to be able to spot this guy, for some reason.

As the members of the team separated with their individual tasks in hand, Dave returned to his desk to mull over what he knew. There on his desk he found the forensic report for the murder of Jamie Peterson. For the next twenty minutes, he scanned the report looking for something that was unusual.

The report stated that death was caused by a shot to the head. Although there was no bullet found, the initial injury did not kill him. Death was caused by a complete breakdown of the person's nervous system due to the introduction of a, as yet unknown poison.

From fragment that were found inside the skull, it would appear that the deceased had been shot by something that resembled a round pellet. Which must have been shot out at a very high velocity for it to have penetrated the skull in that way.

Initial reports are that the pellet probably had a hollow middle filled with a poison. When the pellet broke up on entering the skull, the poison then was able to attack the body's nervous system resulting in a quick but possibly agonising death.

All of the other findings were normal for a man of his age.

This report made Dave feel uneasy.

 "Why had someone gone to all this trouble to kill this man? He knew that both of the families involved were guilty at some time of being responsible for the murder of more than one person. Although none of the family members were ever convicted for murder, in each case the choice of weapon was either a knife or a gun. I can't believe that either one of them would go to these extreme lengths to kill the other when they know how to cover their tracks so successfully. If the two families are not responsible for this crime, then who is and was the deceased the intended victim or not?" thought Dave.

With the report on the desk in front of him, Dave picked up the telephone and asked the operator to put him through to the St Ives Police Station in Cornwall. It wasn't long before the ringing tone could be heard on the other end of the phone.

"Hello, St Ives Police Station, SGT Wilson speaking," said the voice on the other end of the phone.

"Hello SGT, this is DCI Geraint calling from New Scotland Yard. I was wondering if you have someone that I could talk to regarding any unusual occurring deaths recently."

"I'm sorry sir but the only person that could possibly answer your request that is still on duty is me!" replied SGT Wilson.

"Well that will do just with me," said Dave, as he thought back to when he had worked for a while over on the Isle of Wight. Even there it was only to, often that it was left to the lower ranks to hold the fort, so to speak. "Right then, what I'm after is any information regarding any murders or unexplained deaths down there, let's say, over the past two weeks or so!"

"If you can hold on then I will have a look through the book for you sir."

The line went quiet apart from the sounds of pages in a book being turned over and over. That to Dave meant one of two things, either this man was looking hard for the information that he needed. Or, he was just sitting there reading a book quickly while he was being kept hanging on!

"Right sir, I believe that I might have the information that you require," said the Sgt.

"Well according to these reports there were three murders that occurred in just the one week.

First, there was a Mr Joseph Weeks aged 29, who lived and was shot in St Just on the Tuesday.

Second, there was a Carol Innes aged 24, from Porthtowan who was shot in the back.

Third, there was Mr Jamie Peterson aged 40, from London and he was shot in the head in St Ives."

"Bloody hell you seem to have more murders than we do up here in the smoke!" said Dave. "I wonder if I was to give you our Fax No. Would you send copies of the details surrounding their deaths along with copies of any of the forensic reports to me?"

"Yes sir, I'm sure that it would be alright for me to do that. In fact, as it is quite quiet right now I will get straight on with it for you!" replied Sgt Wilson.

Dave then read out the Fax No, then thanked him for all of his help the replaced the receiver. Then armed with a hot mug of strong coffee, Dave sat down to reflect on what he had just heard.

As he sipped his coffee, this thought drifted back to when he had been down in Cornwall that very same week when all of these deaths had occurred. In fact, when he thought even harder, he had been in the very same places on the very same days that all of these murders had been committed!

Was all of this a coincidence or had the intended victim actually been him. This was a sobering thought and he now wondered if the sudden disappearance of his old friend Bill and his wife and son had something to do with all of this?

"Surely if someone wanted to kill me, why would they create such mayhem for all of those other families if the intended victim was me?" thought Dave solemnly.

By the time, he had finished his coffee the fax from Cornwall had come through and was now lying on his desk. After reading through it, Dave came to a very sobering conclusion and that was that he had been the intended victim all along. Why these other people had lost their lives, was either down to the killer being a crap shot or he actually wanted to kill for killing sake!

Armed with this knowledge, Dave knew that he had to take the information up to a much higher level for both guidance and more expertise if required to be brought in from outside to assist in capturing the perpetrator before he commits any more murders.

6

Standing outside, the Chief Constables office, Dave went through his usual ritual. This consisted of making sure that his tie was straight and then rubbing the toes of his shoes on the back of his trousers making sure that they looked clean.

When he was happy with his appearance, he knocked on the door. Instantly there came back a reply of, "Enter!"

Dave opened the door and saw a female who was aged about forty-five years of age. He knew from his past experience of being in this office that this woman was the CC's Personal Assistant or PA as she is commonly referred.

"Yes, can I help you?" said the PA, looking directly at Dave.

"I am DCI Geraint and I urgently need to see the CC as it could be the matter of life or death for one or more police officers in this division!"

Without a second glance at Dave, the PA buzzed through on her intercom and relayed Dave's message.

"Send him through, will you," said a man's voice over the speaker.

With that, the PA gestured to Dave to proceed to the CC's doorway. Dave knocked and then entered the room. In front of him sitting behind a rather large desk was a familiar face. It was Phillip Dobson, he used to be the ACC at the Yard but had recently been promoted in situ up to the dizzy heights of CC.

"Tell me DCI Geraint how are things with you nowadays?" asked the CC, directing Dave towards the seat in front of his desk.

"Well up until today all had been well as far as I was aware. But certain things have since come together that has a worrying tinge to them and I would like to run the scenario passed you and see if you come up with the same result as I do?"

CC Dobson looked intrigued by Dave's statement and listened intently to him as he revealed all of his latest information to him.

"So let me recap the situation as I now see it," said the CC. "You say that when you were on holiday down in Cornwall last week. Three murders were committed and in every case you had been in the exact place when they had occurred."

"Yes," said Dave.

"These three murdered people though had no apparent connection with one another, only that they were shot by the very same calibre ammunition. Also from what you are telling me is that this though is no ordinary bullet, but is a specially designed hollow pellet that has some type of nerve toxin inside it!" said the CC while shaking his head in almost disbelief. "Are you sure of all this, because from where I am sitting, it almost seems like a bizarre scenario that had come from a James Bond movie and not from a real life massacre?"

"What I have told you is correct sir and yes you couldn't make this sort of thing up as it is so unreal. However, there is one of the victims though that could throw a spanner in to the works, if the culprit who committed these murders is not caught quickly. That is how the family of Jamie Peterson, who was the last victim to be killed, react to his murder. As you know that is one of the two main underworld families that are responsible for most of the prostitution and gambling rackets in the Capital. The Peterson family are blaming the Dyer family for the brother's murder. If, they are allowed to retaliate, then we could have a blood bath on the streets of London very soon and that would be disastrous for everyone concerned." replied Dave. "But on top of that, DI Spears and his family are all missing and where ever I have been today interviewing people, my driver has noticed the same person watching us. Now normally I would have dismissed the latter as just coincidence but if you put it along with all of the other information it doesn't make for good reading in my book, sir!"

"Mmm, I can see what you mean," replied the CC. "This is very interesting, seeing as I was wanting to have a word with DI Spears myself today but that is something that will obviously have to wait. So, first things first, what is it that you would want me to do for you?"

"Well first of all I would like you to liaise with the Cornwall Police Authority and request that we take over the investigation, bearing in mind the underworld connections. Then if you could arrange for a police driver named Tom Jukes, to be temporarily assigned to drive me, as he is the only one that can recognise the man who has been watching me! Last of all, I would like you to arrange for someone to gain entry into DI Spears home and make an inspection of the place to look for any answer as to where he and his family have gone to?" said Dave.

"Wouldn't you prefer to make that inspection yourself?" asked the CC.

"No sir, I strongly believe that they are not actually there. However, when all of these snippets of information finally come together, and if we can get a hold of that illusive man? I believe that the answers will finally fall into place. I only hope that we are in time to solve this riddle before another life is lost!" replied Dave standing up.

Dave then left the CC's office and returned to his own.

7

"I need to go and see the Peterson family before they decide to take matters into their own hands," thought Dave picking up the phone and arranging for his driver to meet him at the rear of the building.

The journey across to the Petersons residence was uneventful, apart from Tom the driver thanking Dave for requesting him to be his driver.

Outside the front gates of the Peterson home, Dave told Tom to be extra vigilant while he was inside and to keep a sharp lookout for that strange looking bearded man again. At the front door to the home, Dave rang the doorbell and when the front door opened he was greeted by Sonya, the wife of the deceased. In the lounge while sitting down Dave tried to explain his theory about the untimely murder of her husband. It was at that time when the door to the room opened and their stood Frankie Peterson Jamie's brother.

"What are you doing back here?" he snapped as he walked across to where Dave was sitting.

"DCI Geraint was just trying to explain his theory as to how Jamie was killed," said Sonya as she stood up and stepped between the two men.

"This I have got to hear for myself!" said Frankie standing there with his arms folded. "But I bet that he doesn't have any of the Dyers in the frame for his murder, do you copper!"

Dave took a deep breath and composed himself then said, "Look, I have come here to try to explain my theory as to why Jamie was killed! All I ask is that you listen to what I have to say and then we can take things from there."

Frankie scowled at Dave as he was coerced into sitting down next to Sonya. "Please will you proceed with what you want to tell us?"

Dave then explained about the three people that had all been killed, in the same area of Cornwall in the exact same week using the very same type of method. He then also told them about the stranger that had been seen several times watching him, while he was conducting his investigations. "This person that has been watching me wouldn't have been one of your men by any chance?" asked Dave looking directly at Frankie.

"And what do you mean by that?" said Frankie standing up and standing in a threatening manner.

"Oh, I didn't mean anything," replied Dave staying very calm and remaining seated. "The only reason for me to ask you that was that if it was one of your men, then I wouldn't have to waste valuable time looking for him. That's all!"

"Well I can tell you now, that this person whoever he is. Is not one of my men!" said Frankie starting to calm down.

"Thank you for that," replied Dave standing up. "There is one more thing though and that is while this investigation is underway. The last thing that is needed is a blood bath vendetta going on between the Dyer family and yours. Because I am almost certain that, they had nothing to do with Jamie's murder and if you give me some time and space to work in. Then I hope to be able to prove it to you once and for all!"

Frankie made no reply to what Dave had just said but in this type of place, that response could almost be taken as a maybe!

"I'll show you to the door," said Sonya laying her hand on Frankie as she walked past him.

Nothing more was said as the two made their way to the front door. At the door, Dave thanked her for listening to what he had to say. Then he returned to the waiting police car.

"Where to now sir?" asked Tom.

"Back to the Yard," replied Dave sitting back in the seat and reflecting what had just occurred.

As the police car turned out onto the road, Tom suddenly said aloud, "Oh that bearded man was here again, looking through the front gates."

"Did you manage to get a better look at him this time?" replied Dave sitting forward in his seat.

"Oh I did one better that that!" said Tom smugly. "I managed to take his picture on my mobile phone!"

"Quick, pull over and let me have a look at it!" said Dave all eagerly.

Tom found a safe place to stop and then located the picture on hid phone and handed it to Dave.

"I tried to zoom, the picture in as far as my camera would let me," said Tom. "That is about the best that I could get it this time!"

Dave stared at the tiny picture that clearly showed the bearded man looking through the barred gates. Unfortunately, though, he was still too far away, for him to be clearly recognised from that picture.

"Well done you!" said Dave, clearly excited that finally he had proof that this person really existed. "When we get back to the Yard, I will have this photo blown up by the tech boys and we will see if they are as good as they are always saying they are!"

The trip back to the Scotland Yard was for the first time a more light-hearted journey.

———

8

Bill began to stir from a deep sleep, when he suddenly could feel something blowing air onto his face. He was about to stretch out with his hands when he remembered about the pack of wolves, waiting to try to eat him down below the small ledge where he was now lying.

"Was this blowing of air on his face from one of the wolves, or was it from something else?" thought Bill, as he slowly opened up one of his eyes to take a look.

With a part of him wanting to know his fate and the other part fighting against it, Bill finally plucked up the courage to see. Peeping through the eyelashes on the cracked open eyelids, Bill scanned the area as much as he could without moving his head from side to side. When the coast looked clear and there was no sign of there being a wolf standing over him. Bill raised himself up onto his elbows so that he was able to have another look about him.

Down on the floor of the cave, there were no signs of the pack of wolves that had been there last night.

"I wonder if they have gone?" thought Bill craning his neck to look as far around the cave as he thought would be safe to do so. After seeing no sign of any of the wolves, Bill turned his body and swung his feet out and over the side of the ledge so that he could sit up straight.

"Well if it wasn't from the wolves, where was that cool breeze coming from?" thought Bill. "Because it isn't blowing on my legs so that it can't be coming in through the cave opening."

Bill looked above him but could not tell from which direction the breeze was coming from. So he wet his finger and held it up in the air. Soon he was able to pinpoint from which direction it was coming from. Although Bill could not see any gap above him, he knew that there must be one for the breeze to blow down through it. He decided to take a look for himself and pulled up his good right leg ready to try to stand up. As he was doing that, he heard a noise coming from below. Bill stopped what he was doing and gazed once more down onto the cave floor only to see the white teeth and the huge head of a wolf leaping up the side of the cave wall towards his left foot.

Instinctively, Bill drew his foot up just before the wolf could lock his sharp teeth onto it. Then as if on springs, Bills feet sprang up beneath him enabling him to stand up on the ledge. With the wolves now snapping and growling beneath him. Bill took the opportunity to see what was above his head.

It was while looking for a way out that his thoughts turned to his wife Rosalynd and his son Sammy. What had happened to them and where were they both now? That was a turning point for Bill and he knew then that he must battle on to try to escape from this place and get some help to save his family from whatever danger at this moment they were in to. With that thought in mind, Bill refocused his attention on trying to make his escape and try to find them.

Looking up at first, he could see nothing that could help him escape from those animals below. Then after reaching above him, he could feel yet another ledge, which appeared to be larger than the one he was standing on.

Now he was in a quandary, does he try to climb up, or should he stay where he is and hope that the wolf pack would go away?

The answer came when he heard yet another attempt to reach him by yet another one of the wolves. This time though, he seemed to be getting much further up the side of the cave and closer to the ledge that he was on. Bill decided that his only chance of survival was to try to climb up and hope to find where the air was coming in. Whether the opening would be large enough for him to get through though, would be another thing!

So standing on his good foot and using his injured foot as a balance. Bill tried hopping up high enough for him to gain any type of purchase on the surface to enable him to pull himself up and out of danger. The first couple of attempts failed, in fact the one time he almost fell completely off the ledge itself. Finally, he was able to gain enough momentum to clamber up onto the higher ledge and then take a rest. While he lay there looking all around, he could still hear the sounds of the wolf pack trying to scale the cave wall. At least now, he knew that they could not reach him where he was. However, if he could not find a way out from there, he would also be trapped as the way down would almost certain result in further injury or even death if he was to fall off the ledge to the floor below.

When he had managed to regain his breath, Bill reached around above his head looking for a gap for him to escape through. Eventually, he was able to force his hand through a thin covering of dirt and grass that had somehow managed to cover the opening over many years. It took a while but soon an opening was made that was large enough for him to climb through. Out of the cave and lying on the ground for the first time felt great for Bill. He had finally eluded the wolf packs, who still think that he's above them waiting to be eaten.

His elation though was short lived as the icy wind bit into his body like sharp needles.

"Here I go again," though Bill looking around him. "If I don't find somewhere else that is out of this wind then I might as well have stayed in the cave and been, at least warmer. Well at last it looks as though my injured foot has finally stopped bleeding, so that is one less thing for me to worry about!"

So, with the fleece wrapped around him, Bill walked off into the unknown looking for shelter and or help to escape this nightmare. All the time he was walking, Bill kept listening out for any signs of the wolf pack. Then, something that being carried on the icy breeze, hit Bill in the face startling him. Instinctively, Bill raised his hand up to his face to wipe whatever it was quickly away. As he did this, he was hit by several more things. These though began to hurt as they collided with his skin.

Bill looked out into the distance and to his horror he realised that what had been hitting him was snow. In the distance, he could see a white blanket of snow heading his way. Mixed with the snow were particles of hail and they felt like needles, when they came into contact with Bill's skin.

"How much fucking more have I got to deal with before I'm allowed to be free of this place?" shouted Bill at the top of his voice.

The feeling of despair now engrossed Bill as he dropped onto the cols ground and tears welled up in his eyes and finally overflowed, running down his cheeks and dripping down onto the ground.

"Why am I here and who has put me here? Cried out Bill holding his hands outstretched and looking skywards. "If I only knew that my family were safe, then I could let this hell hole of a place finish me off!"

As Bill's state of mind dropped lower and lower and the feeling of complete hopelessness drifted across him. Through the swirling snow, in the distance, a shape became visible.

"Bloody hell, is that a house over there?" said Bill to himself. He forced himself to stand up for a better look and wiped the snow from his eyes.

"Yes, I do believe that it is a house or something like one at least," said Bill aloud.

Keeping heading in that direction, Bill soon found himself nearing what looked like an old wooden shack. He located the door and banged hard on it. When there was no response, he lifted the latch on the door and stepped inside. With the door closed, the icy blast of wind was no more. As Bill looked around the single room, he saw what looked like an old ram shackled wooden bed over in the corner. There were some shelving on one of the walls and in the middle of the room was an old style wood burning heater.

"Great, I've got a wood burner in a place that appears to have no trees!" shouted Bill aloud.

In the corner, Bill found some old wooden chairs and something that used to be a type of hand-made table once. He managed to break them up into pieces that were small enough to fit inside the heater. Then he looked around for something to light it, unfortunately that was where his luck ran out. Despair then began to creep in as he rummaged through the shack looking for matches or anything that would cause a spark so that he could be able to light the fire and get warm.

Up on one of the shelves, Bill came across an old oil lamp and took it down for a closer look. Although there was no oil left inside the lamp, he did find two oddly shaped sharp stones seated on top of the lamp.

"That's unusual," thought Bill picking up the stones for a closer look. "I wonder why they were left there like that."

He held the stones in his hands for a closer look, then, he noticed that when the light caught them at certain angles they both gave off an unusual sheen.

"I wonder if these stones are in fact pieces of flint and that is why they were being kept on top of that lamp?" thought Bill, as he began rubbing the two stones together.

After a few attempts, sparks were coming from the striking stones. Putting the stones down carefully, so that they did not become lost, Bill looked around for anything that would be easily set fire to. He gathered up as much tinder dry bits of fabric and placed them on the base of the burner. Bill then tried hard to set fire to the rags but to no avail. Sitting back on the bed, he tried to think of anything that he could see that might set alight more easily.

"Ah, I wonder if that would work?" said Bill standing up.

A few minutes later Bill was sitting in front of the wood burner for another attempt at lighting a fire. Time after time, he struck the two stones together without any success. Then literally, in a flash, a flame could be seen filtering down towards the rags getting bigger as got nearer to them. After a little coaxing by Bill blowing gently on the flame, the pieces of rag finally caught fire. Bill then added some small sticks of wood until the fire was strong enough for him to be able to put on some bigger pieces.

Now sitting on the bed in front of a flaming fire, Bill for the first time in ages began to feel warm again. With heat now permeating through his entire body, Bill reached out and picked up an old dirty metal tin. With the tin in hand, Bill looked out through the dirty window and saw that the snow had begun to settle on the ground. He opened the door just enough for him to reach out and using the tin can, scoop up a tin full of snow, and returned back to the wood burner.

Once there, Bill placed the tin on top of the stove and then sat back and watched it melt into a piping hot drink.

"Who would have thought that that huge pile of old cobwebs would have burnt enough for me to light this fire!" said Bill out loud.

He then took time to reflect on his situation as the heat from the fire filtered through his body, warming it right to its core. His sense of despair began to drift away, as pleasant thoughts of Rosalynd and little Sammy re-entered his head. Now instead of being alone, at least in spirit, he felt for the first time in ages that his family were all back together.

Using some of the old rags, Bill took the hot tin off the burner and began to take his first hot sips of liquid in days.

9

At the Yard, Dave told Tom to take his mobile phone along to the tech boys and get them to make a blow up of the bearded man's picture. While on his desk, were some written reports about the movements of both the Peterson and the Dyer families?

"Well according to these reports, there has not been any physical connection between the two warring families yet! So that at least is something to be thankful for," thought Dave as he made himself a cup of coffee.

While he drank his coffee, Dave's thoughts moved to what type of gun would be used to fire that particular type of ammunition to cause such damage. He phoned the forensic laboratory looking for some answers. They in turn had been in touch with a gun specialist looking for the very same answers. He had told them that the weapon would most likely be a long barrelled gun very much like an air pistol. They believed though that this gun would need to be combined with a gas cartridge of some type to give it the power required to penetrate the skull in that way. The design however could be that of a walking stick or an actual rifle. That, unfortunately, is the one question that cannot be answered easily until the actual gun is found!

Putting down the phone, Dave then looked back through the records that had been made when the other people had been killed. The one constant thing was the fact that there had been no reports of any gunfire in every reported incident.

"Well I think that the idea of a specially made gun that is somehow powered by a gas canister is looking more and more likely," thought Dave as he dropped the reports back down onto his desk. Just then, the door to his office opened and through it came, Tom the driver with something big held under his armpit.

"And what have you got there?" asked Dave pointing to his arm.

"This is the blown up picture from my mobile," said Tom eagerly, as he laid the photo out on top of Dave's desk and stood back so that he could take a closer look at it.

"So, this is our mystery bearded man then!" said Dave moving to the side so that Tom could take a closer look.

"Yes sir that is him!"

"Mmm, I wonder just who you are and more importantly why are you so interested in where I am going to?" said Dave.

Even after scrutinizing the man in the pictures face. Bill still had no idea as to who this person was or what was his part in all of this. The one thing that he was sure of was that whoever this person is, the police must somehow get to him, before any members of the Peterson or Dyer families do!

Dave's desk was now becoming covered with files and reports that all in some way had to do with this case. There was the one from the CC, informing him that after talking with the Cornwall CC, with regards to the three murders. They have agreed that he could be in control of the investigation as long as they were kept informed of any developments. Then there was the report about the teams that had gone to Bill's home and had a look through it for any clues as to where he, his wife and child had all disappeared to.

The outcome was greeted with mixed emotions from Dave. On the one hand, he was pleased that they had found nothing untoward inside the home. That meant that they could all still be alive somewhere. That though then raised even more questions primarily being, why are they all missing also where the hell are they now?

10

Picking up the phone, Dave asked that his driver be ready for him downstairs in ten minutes.

This time, Dave went and sat in the front passenger seat next to Tom. Dave then told Tom the driver to head back to the DOG & DUCK pub. On the journey to the pub, Dave told Tom to keep a sharp lookout for the bearded man. As they neared the area where the pub was, Dave told Tom to slow the car down so that they could take in who was around them.

Pulling up outside the DOG & Duck public house, they both just sat there looking all around hoping to see the bearded man again. Where the old pub stood, was on the edge of the old part of London and where it bordered with the new. The road where they had parked was across the road from a relatively new shopping complex. This whole area, used to be quite run down with most of the old properties standing empty and in a state of disrepair. Now though, after a large building development including new housing along with this smart new multi-tiered shopping centre had been completed, the, tone of the area had risen tenfold over the past couple of years.

Where this road had once been a very narrow single carriageway, it now boasted four lanes for the traffic, two in either direction with a pedestrian foot bridge now spanning across the roadway.

"What makes you think that he will be around here?" asked Tom, not taking his eyes off the streets for one second.

"That is a good question," replied Dave doing the same as Tom. "What I would like to know is how did he know in advance, that I was going to be in all of those places in the first place?"

"Don't look now sir, but I do believe that, that is our bearded over there!" said Tom nudging Dave and pointing out the direction for him to look.

Dave casually turned his head to look as directed and sure enough, there standing across the road from them, was the mysterious bearded man. As their eyes met, there was no reaction from the man who was just standing there with his walking stick.

"Shall I get out and go and have a word with him for you sir," asked Tom opening the cars door.

Dave turned, and was about to reply when there was a loud crack sound on his side window of the police car. It was as if time had stopped and everything was travelling in slow motion. When the loud crack was heard inside the car. Dave immediately turned back to his left, and looked directly towards the bearded man and saw that he had his walking stick pointed at them. The car's side window was now cracked directly in line with Dave's head, where something must have hit it at great speed. Tom had stopped getting out of the car and appeared almost paralyzed, stopping half in and half out of the car.

"Quick, get back in the car Tom!" shouted Dave keeping his eyes firmly on the bearded man. "Christ almighty, he's shooting at us. Quick, get back inside and drive this bloody car straight at that bastard!"

Tom, without uttering another word, automatically dropped back into the driver's seat and turned the ignition key. The powerful engine roared into life and Tom turned the wheel hard to the left and floored the accelerator driving the police car at a fast pace towards the man. Although the distance was only a short one, Both Dave and Tom could clearly see the bearded man trying hard to reload the gun, which had been cleverly disguised as a walking stick. As the police car drove at right angles to the other traffic that were on the road. There were loud squeals from the tyres as the other drivers frantically braked hard to avoid colliding with them. Car horns were being blasted, along with some shouts of abuse from some of the irate drivers. None of this though deterred Tom from doing what he had been told. The people that were close to the bearded man seemed to part just like the pictures of the Red Sea in the Bible. Once again, there was a loud crack as something this time bounced off the cars windscreen, making it crack all the way across.

"Run that fucking bastard down!" shouted Dave, his eyes almost transfixed on the man.

Bang, crash!

The police cars wheels hit the curbed edge of the pavement making the front of the vehicle bounce high into the air. This briefly obstructed their view of the bearded man. However, when the front of the car dropped back down again, the bearded man was now nowhere to be seen.

Dave and Tom leapt out of the police car hoping to catch a glimpse of their suspect. But once again he had managed to evade them.

"What's the matter with you?" shouted one of the members of the public that had just had to flee for their lives to avoid being run down.

"I'm sorry sir for your fright but did you happen to see where that beaded man went too?" said Dave still looking all around him.

"Oh you try to run us all down and then you want us to help you to find someone," replied a male passer-by trying to gee up some support from the now gathering crowd.

Dave now had a much different problem to try to solve and that was how to pacify irate members of the public without losing his suspect.

"I wonder sir; could I have a word with you for a second over here!" said Dave to the irate man.

"Why, are you going to arrest me for shouting out just now?"

"No, on the contrary, I would just like to try and explain to you what was happening to make us take the action that we did?" said Dave calmly.

"Well, what do you think?" shouted the man to the surrounding crowd of people.

Mutters and silly quips were thrown back towards him and finally he agreed to move away from the main crowd of people and allow Dave to speak to him.

"Look, the only reason for our actions just then was to hopefully prevent any loss of life. The person that we were driving towards was wanted for killing people and had just fired at us while we were sitting in that police car!" said Dave pointing towards the broken windows on the car.

The man glanced back at the police car and then replied in a smug tone of voice, "Look copper, I wouldn't help you under any circumstances!"

This reaction was not what Dave expected to hear and it was not going to help him to catch up with their suspect any sooner. "Tell me sir, are you here shopping on your own or are you just waiting for someone?"

The man looked strangely at Dave then replied, "Why, what's that got to do with you?"

"Oh I'm just curious that's all," said Dave looking straight at the man. "Well!"

"If you must know, I am waiting for my wife and little girl to finish doing some shopping in there," replied the man pointing towards the new shopping complex.

"That's very interesting?" said Dave, looking up at the shopping complex. "Because, I have a very strong suspicion that our armed gunman, has gone into that very same place where your family are, to avoid being caught by me. So you see your silly display here might just be placing your family in danger, just so that you can get one over the police"

That statement hit home hard and resulted in the man's face draining of all colour. "That man did go into there, I watched him go through those doors over there," stammered the man as the realisation of his actions hit home.

11

Dave immediately took out his mobile and called up the police control room. "This is DCI Geraint. I urgently need armed police back up at the shopping complex that is opposite the DOG & Duck public house. I will be going directly to their security room and they can meet up with me there."

Dave then called to Tom and they both ran towards the main doors that lead into the huge shopping complex. Inside the concourse of the building, Dave's eyes looked all around. In front of him was a wide sprawling area filled with members of the public. To both sides there were slightly curved stairs that lead the shoppers up to the upper level of the complex. All around the outer walls of the upper floor, were various types of shops all trying their best to entice punters in to buy their goods?

It was a similar design below except that there were several bench type seats that were scattered about for the weary shoppers to rest their aching feet before setting off shopping yet again. This was an ideal place for someone to conceal themselves and to be able to fire at them unseen and with all of the noise, totally unheard.

"Tom, you stay close to me at all times, do you hear!" said Dave as he noticed a uniformed security guard standing just to the left of the concourse. "While I speak to this guard, I need you to keep a sharp lookout for our bearded suspect. Remember, he has already fired his weapon twice at both of us today, so stay alert!"

"Hello there, I am DCI Geraint from Scotland Yard. A few minutes ago a bearded man entered through these doors and I wondered if you saw him?"

"Are you taking the piss?" replied the guard. "How do you expect me to remember everyone that has entered here?"

"Look, can you get hold of you man in charge of security quickly!" said Dave looking all around for any glimpse of their man.

"If I didn't see him, why the hell would he have!" replied the guard, in a blasé manner.

Dave was not very happy with the attitude of this man and after giving out a loud sigh; he moved closer to him and whispered in his ear, "Look you useless bag of shit, the person that entered here just now, is armed and very dangerous. We already know that he has killed at least three people in cold blood and tried to shoot both of us outside here. If you don't get on your fucking radio and get hold of someone that can assist me in locating him before someone else is killed, then I'll have you arrested for police obstruction. In addition, in the very likely event that another person should lose their life while you a farting about, you could be held as an accomplice before and after that fact, have I made myself very clear to you?"

"Yes sir," replied the guard speaking on his radio.

Valuable minutes passed by before the head of the security arrived to assist Dave. In fact, he arrived virtually at the very same time as the armed response team entered the building.

"Who's in charge here?" said one of the armed police officers.

"That would be me," replied Dave. "I am DCI Geraint from the Yard and we have an armed suspect inside this building. He's armed with what looks like an ordinary walking stick but in fact, it is a deadly weapon. When fired there is no detectable sound as the mechanism is generated via a small gas cartridge. Somehow we need to seal off this entire complex and then make a search of the entire premises for our bearded man," said Dave to the men that were standing around him. "Make no mistake. This person will have no compunction about shooting you or anyone else that should get in his way. What I want to try and do first is to lock down this entire building and to move all the members of the public outside for their own safety."

"But this is a very busy time," replied the head of security.

"Oh ok," said Dave, "Then you can have the unenviable job of informing their family members if one of them is killed due to the fact that you don't want to stop these people from shopping!"

That quick response from Dave brought a smile to some of the armed police officers that were standing around.

"I am Inspector Kyle and I am in charge of these men."

"It's good to have you around just now," replied Dave. "The one thing that I will tell you is that the main intended victim for this gunman is actually me!"

"Why you sir?" asked Inspector Kyle.

"Ah well that question still evades me for the time being," said Dave. "So I'm really hoping that catching this man might throw some light onto more than one problematic thing that is not really quite right!"

"Well we will have to try and take him alive then, won't we!" replied the inspector with a wry smile on his face.

"Now that would be helpful but not at the expense of another potential loss of life, you understand?" said Dave.

"Do I understand that if it is deemed necessary, then we have a green light to take him down if he threatens to kill again!" said Inspector Kyle, listening intently to Dave reply.

"Yes, you have a green light if you believe that loss of life is imminent," said Dave. "And I will back you up, if it should come to that!"

With his instructions now, Chrystal clear, the inspector along with the security guards began the task of emptying the shopping area. This was made easier, due to the fact that, there were only two ways to either enter or exit the place. So with the security guards ushering the shoppers out of the building being backed up by armed police. There were very few complaints from the members of the public. Those that did want to complain about their treatment, were advised to cooperate, if only for the safety of them and their family members. When they realised that their family could be at risk by remaining, they soon opted for the safe alternative and quickly left the building.

It took less than an hour to clear the majority of people out of the area. Those that still remained, were up on the upper floor. Then over the police radio, Dave received a call from Inspector Kyle.

"Sir, we have a situation on the upper floor where we believe that your man is held up in one of the shops. A woman has managed to escape from out of the shoe shop concerned and informed us that there is a man acting very strangely inside. What do you want us to do?"

"Is the shop contained by your men?" asked Dave.

"Yes, and according to the woman who happens to be the manageress of the shop. That there is only one way in or out of the shop and that is via the front door," said Inspector Kyle.

"Right, do not try to enter the shop until I arrive. Meanwhile keep everyone clear and I will be along shortly," said Dave, taking a deep breath and heading up the stairs.

At the top of the stairs, Dave, was met by one of the armed officers who then guided him across to where the inspector was waiting. "I take it that there are no security guards still around here!" said Dave trying to eye up the situation.

"No, I have instructed them to remain downstairs seeing as all of the other shops are now clear!" said Inspector Kyle.

"Do we have such a thing as a megaphone handy?" asked Dave.

In an instant one was produced and he familiarised himself as to how it worked. "It's alright," said Dave when he noticed the inspector watching him fiddle with its controls. "I had an embarrassing moment once with one of these things; I began speaking and had been rambling on for ages when someone informed me that I had forgotten to keep the button pressed when speaking. It took an age for me to live that thing down, so that is why I am making sure that I get things right this time!"

That admission from the DCI brought a smile to a few of the armed police officers as they remembered when they too had made the same mistake at some time or another.

"You in the shoe shop. This is Detective Chief Inspector Geraint and I would like to speak to whoever is inside the shop. I will tell you that with me are armed police officers and that the only way out of those premises are through the front door."

From inside the shop, faint sounds could be heard as if boxes were being thrown about, then after several minutes had passed a female called out. "Please, don't come in, otherwise he says that he will kill me and you!"

"Are you alright?" asked Dave calmly. "Yes, so far but he is holding a hand gun to my head!" said the frightened woman.

"Now that's interesting," said Dave to the inspector. "Until now, we thought that he only had a homemade rifle that had been designed to look like it was a walking stick. Now it seems that he has gotten hold of a handgun as well! I think that you should update your men to that fact, so that they are not taken by surprise if he should try to make a break for it!"

"This is to the man that is in the shop. What is it that you want?" said Dave trying to discover the man's real intentions.

Once again, after a few minutes it was the female that replied, "He says that he wants you all to go away and he be allowed to leave here!"

Dave knew that he could not allow this to happen but delayed his response while he thought about his next move. Dave then took Inspector Kyle to one side and had a brief discussion with him about the situation. Then they both returned and Dave once again picked up the megaphone and said, "Right, if you can give me a few minutes, then I will clear the area of armed police and you can then come out and have a talk with me man to man."

"If this is some sort of a trick, he says that he will kill me first and then you!" said the frightened female hostage.

"Look, I'm sure that you both are able to get into a position while still inside the shop, to enable the person that is in there with you to see out and confirm that the police have all gone away and that I am the only one remaining," said Dave moving to stand in full view of the shop window. He knew that he was this man's real target and he was hoping that having the opportunity to shoot Dave would be too much of an offer for the man to refuse.

Suddenly Dave could hear movement coming from inside the shoe shop. This was an anxious time for Dave, as he wondered, did this person just want to shoot and kill him, or did he actually want to be present when he committed the final act. Then Dave's thoughts vanished from his mind when he saw two figures inside the shop moving towards the front door. It was the bearded man and he was holding a female in front of him. As they slowly made their way closer to the front of the shop, Dave could just make out the shape of a gun pressed against the young woman's neck.

"It's alright, all of the police have moved away," called Dave to the man. "As you can see, I am not armed so you are completely safe!"

The man did not reply but kept moving closer to the doorway all the time scanning from side to side looking to see if he could see anyone. Eventually, the man and his hostage were both standing in the doorway of the shop, facing Dave.

"Can you tell me your name?" said Dave. "That way then, at least I will know what to call you!"

The man just smiled when he heard what Dave had just said. "You have no idea who I am yet do you?" said the bearded man, pressing his head closer to the back of the young woman's head.

"No, you are right, I have no idea who you are or why you want to kill me?" replied Dave feeling very uneasy. "Can I take it that we have met before at some time?"

"Oh yes, we've met before and you already know what my name is?" replied the man almost sniggering at Dave's inability to recognise him. "By the way, I wonder how your partner is surviving his ordeal. I should let you know that if anything should happen to me, then his fate will be sealed along with mine. He is only still alive due to my intervention and only I know where he is right now!"

"Why are you doing this?" asked Dave trying to glean some more information from the man. "And what did we do that requires both of us to lose our lives in this way?"

The man lowered his head as if remembering something. Then he became enraged and shouted to Dave, "You took something precious from me and now you will both have to pay the ultimate price. With that, the bearded man pushed the frightened woman to his left and down onto the floor, then raised the gun up in front of him and took careful aim at Dave. For a split second, Dave stood there looking down the barrel of a handgun with thoughts racing through his head, trying hard to think who was this person and where in God's name was Bill and his family?

The whole area fell silent as Dave and the bearded man stood face to face with only one of them knowing the truth that had lead them to this place. Then suddenly there was a loud BANG!

12

"Sir, are you alright?" said a man's voice.

Slowly Dave's eyes opened and there standing in front of him were Tom and Inspector Kyle. "Are you injured in any way?" asked the inspector sounding concerned.

Dave gingerly felt all over his body and then in a very relieved tone of voice replied, "No, it would appear that he missed me!"

"No, the only reason that he missed you was due to the fact that one of my men realised his intention to fire and he acted accordingly and took the man out prior to him being able to discharge his weapon at you. Unfortunately, though, he was hence killed in the process," said the inspector.

Tom helped a shocked Dave to lean against the walkway handrail.

"I know that it is a pathetic thing to say, but just closed my eyes when I realised that he was about to pull the trigger and shoot me!" said Dave to the inspector.

"Don't you worry about that; I believe that if I had been standing looking down the barrel of a gun that was being held by someone that wanted to kill me. Then I strongly believe that I would have done the same!" said Inspector Kyle smiling broadly.

Once Dave had regained his composure, he moved to have a closer look at the man that wanted to kill him. Now though, he was the one lying dead on the floor surrounded by blood from the fatal head wound that he had received from a police sharpshooter. It was only then, that he remembered the female hostage.

"Is the hostage alright?" asked Dave as his mind and body once more kicked into gear.

"Yes she is fine," replied Inspector Kyle. "Apart from being frightened shitless by that madman. Her only physical injury was on one of her knees, when she was thrown to one side as the gunman took aim at you. At this moment in time, she is being looked after by some ambulance personnel."

Feeling relieved that no one else had come to any harm from the mystery man. Dave made a call arranging for extra police to attend the shopping centre to help keep the area sealed off until the forensic team were finished examining the shop that the gunman had held up in, prior to his death.

"Would you let the forensic chaps know that the homemade weapon is still unaccounted for? We also need to locate that gun before it can fall into the wrong hands. Finally, will you please give my regards to the person that saved me inspector," said Dave still feeling numb inside. "I understand that it is the last thing that anyone wants to have to do. But this time he did it to save a life, my life and I will be forever grateful to him or her for that!"

Dave then shook the inspectors hand and left him to wait for the police backup to arrive. Meanwhile he and Tom went outside the centre for some fresh air.

———————

13

At the morgue, Dave and Tom both waited for the results of the post-mortem.

"I'm sorry that I made you do such a terrible thing today," said Dave placing his right hand down onto Tom's shoulder. "If you would prefer to go home and have a break, then I will understand!"

"No thank you sir," replied Tom still shaking from his ordeal. "But can I ask, are things like this an everyday occurrence with you?"

Dave turned and smiled at that question and replied in an almost laughable tone of voice, "Hell no, even I couldn't put up with that sort of things on a yearly practice never mind on a daily one!"

It was a couple of hours until the autopsy was completed and the results all been written up. The coroner himself brought out the report to Dave himself.

"Well we certainly have a strange one hear Dave?" said the coroner shaking his head.

"Why do you say that?" replied Dave looking a little confused.

"Well if you like then I will give you a precise` of what I have found.

First of all, the man was killed due to a high velocity bullet in the head. Secondly, there was a strange residue found on his hands that was consistent with the ammunition, which, was also found concealed on his person. Thirdly and this is where things are now handed completely over to you. The man concerned was wearing a false wig and full beard?" said the coroner handing over the report to Dave.

"Were there anything of interest found in his clothing?" asked Dave.

"Oh yes, there was a mobile phone, which is now broken. Obviously through making contact with the floor," said the coroner smiling. "Ah and there was also what looks like a front door key but there was no indication as to his address though!"

"Bloody hell!" said Tom aloud. "Tell me sir, did you actually understand all of what that bloke just said then!"

"Unfortunately, yes I did," said Dave looking down at Toms bemused face. "But when you have had to deal with as many of these reports as what I have over the years. You learn to try to keep an open mind, that way nothing tends to amaze you. Now this is where my job can actually begin. Now that we have the man's finger prints then if he is in the system, then it should be easy for us to locate his true identity."

Back at the Yard, the deceased man's fingerprints were entered into the police computer system and all they could do for now was to wait and see what pops up!

It was while Dave along with his driver Tom, were both getting a warm drink out of one of the many vending machines. They were told that they had found an exact match for the fingerprints taken off the now dead bearded man. Dave was then handed some paperwork that had both the bearded man's prints on it, along with the match that had been located. He scanned over the pages until he came to the man's real name. That was when Dave let out a huge sigh of disbelief when he immediately recognised who it was!

"From all accounts, the dead man is already known to me," said Dave to Tom. "His full name is Norman Ferris who should still be in prison for Air Piracy and attempted murder of roughly four hundred passengers on a flight to Australia."

"How do you know this?" asked Tom naively.

"That is because DI Spears and I were the two that caught him and were able to prevent his plan from seeing fruition!" replied Dave as he thought back to the last time that he had seen him. "But how can this person be out of prison so soon? And could he be the real reason behind the disappearance of Bill Spears while all of this has been going on!"

Dave then told Tom to go off and see if he can get another vehicle ready in case he needs to make some more journeys. So while Tom headed off, Dave returned to his office and began making calls to find out more about this man Ferris being released!

After several calls were made from Dave's office, it transpired that according to prison records. Until recently, Norman Ferris, had been incarcerated in Parkhust Prison on the Isle of Wight. When it was somehow brought to governors notice that he was soon going to be due for early release. This they blindly complied with without making any more checks prior to releasing him and Norman Ferris, was consequentially then released from prison, on parole more than two months ago. It wasn't until he failed to keep his appointment with the parole officer, that further checks were made and that was when they found that their computer system had been hacked into and the dates on the prisoner's records had been altered

According to the prison governor at Parkhust, Norman Ferris was allowed as a part of his rehabilitation programme, to go on a computer course inside the prison. Interestingly though, his instructor for most of the time was another inmate by the name of, Jack Wilkinson. The interesting thing about Jack was the fact that he was inside Parkhurst himself, for committing computer fraud in the first place!

When this mistake was located, the prison staff made inspections, and crossed referenced all of the other prisoners' records to make sure that they too hadn't been altered by him. Ironically the only one that they were able to detect that had been altered was that of a certain Jack Wilkinson. His original sentence was set at seven years. When they checked it out, it now read seventeen years! Ferris had even screwed him over as well!

"Well it looks like I may be making a trip down to the Isle of Wight to have a little chat with this Jack Wilkinson" thought Dave as he gathered up his coat and headed off downstairs.

14

The journey from London down to the Island went well although there was not too much in the way of conversation coming from inside the car. Tom, the police driver was finding that he was having to concentrate much more than usual after driving into and killing that man earlier on that day. At first, he wasn't sure that he even wanted to drive a car again but it had been DCI Geraint that had finally convinced him that he should give it a go. After all, he was only obeying Dave's orders at the time, and as he had explained to Tom. If their car had not run him over, then one or even both of them could have been killed by him. So with that thought in mind. Tom decided to give driving one more try, and the trip out of the Capital would be the ideal place to find out if he was right or not!

Pulling up outside Parkhurst Prison, Dave got out of the car and told Tom to wait there for him.

"Don't you want me to come inside with you sir?" asked Tom.

"No!" replied Dave looking up at the high walls that surrounded the prison. "What you have to remember Tom, is that apart from the prison staff. Every other single person that is located behind that wall is only there because a police officer somewhere had managed to feel his collar and get him sent down for a long time. For that, they don't seem to like us too much, ok!"

"Christ, I hadn't thought of it in that way sir," replied Tom, getting back inside the car.

Dave walked across the car park and went into the reception.

"Can I help you sir?" asked a prison officer from behind security glass.

"Yes, I am Detective Chief Inspector Geraint and I have an appointment with your Governor, a Mr Snow I believe."

When confirmation of the appointment was made, Dave was taken through the security barrier and up into the offices where Governor Snow was waiting for him. After a brief discussion about how Norman Ferris had managed to hack into the computer system. Dave was taken through to where special visits take place away from the normal visiting room. He was then shown into the room and informed that someone would be bringing the prisoner, Wilkinson down to see him a.s.a.p.

As Dave entered the room, there was a similar set up that he had seen at previous interviews that he had been involved in? There were high windows set into the walls that you could not see out of. A table was positioned in the centre of the room, with a couple of chairs close by. All around the room was a rubber strip that had been inset inside a thin metal band. This was the alarm push and is only used if the prisoner should become violent and extra help is required to control the situation.

Dave turned to face the door and was surprised to see that the governor was still in the room with him.

"Are you staying while I interview the prisoner?" asked Dave to the governor.

"Yes, well after the cock up had been made under my nose, so to speak. Then the least that I can do is to be available as it is hopefully wrapped up!"

Minutes later, the door to the room opened and a prison officer and another person entered the room.

"Sit down over there Wilkinson, will you?" said the Governor pointing towards the chair.

The man moved across to the chair without speaking and sat down. The prison officer that had brought him moved and took up position alongside the wall where he had a clear view of the prisoner.

"As you already know, I am Mr Snow Governor of Parkhurst. This gentleman is DCI Geraint from New Scotland Yard and he would like to ask you some question with regards to a Norman Ferris!"

Jack Wilkinson looked up at the governor then turned and did the same to Dave. "You won't get anything out of me. You see, none of you can prove that I've done anything wrong?"

Dave moved around the table and got a little closer to the prisoner then said, "Look, all I want to know from you is whether Norman Ferris ever said anything to you about getting his own back on the policemen that had put him inside. That's all!"

A wry smile crept across Jack's face, as he looked straight into Dave's face and replied, "Well if he did tell me anything, then I must have forgot it, oops!"

"Look, all we want to know is will you help the police to find him?" said the governor, almost pleading with him in comply.

"Fuck you and the lot of you!" replied Jack smiling broadly as he realised that whatever Ferris had planned, he must have succeeded otherwise this copper would not be here now else!

A sense of smugness fell across the prisoners face with knowledge that him, knowing something and them proving it is another thing entirely.

"Ok," said Dave moving away from the prisoner's side. "What I can though tell you and you can take what I say now as being fact! You are bordering on being charged as an accessory to three murders and the attempted murder of two policemen."

"You can't do that; cos I've got an alibi for everything that has happened outside this nick. How can I be connected with any of those crimes if I've never left the fucking hole?" said Jack in a smug voice and a silly grin that stretched right across his face.

"Oh that is easy to prove, just though the process of association!" replied Dave looking directly at Jack. "You see, it was only due to the fact that you gave him the knowledge to enable him to get out of this prison and then disappear. That Norman Ferris was able to commit those atrocities! Oh by the way, one of his victims was a prominent family member of one of London's ruling underworld families. When they discover your role in all of this, I have a strong feeling that even these high walls won't be strong enough to be able to protect you from their wrath!"

"You can't tell them about me?" stammered Jack, now minus the smile. "If you tell them my name then you will be sentencing me to death!"

"Oh, God forbid that it would be me or even one of my colleagues that would be responsible for doing such a thing," replied Dave stone faced. "But by now I would be very surprised that someone connected to the family concerned, has not been informed of my appointment at this prison to see only you!"

"You bastard, this, is some sort of a lousy trick just to try and get me to grass on a fellow inmate. Well I don't grass on anyone see copper, so you can just piss off back to London and leave me alone!" shouted Jack.

"Ok, I can understand that you don't want to be known as a grass but do you think that you could tell me something that will not offend your weird sense of loyalty then?" said Dave in a calm tone of voice.

"And what would that be, then?" said Jack with a smirk on his face, enjoying the moment of power that he now appeared to have over them.

"Well from our records, you were sent down for computer fraud. Am I correct so far?" said Dave casually glancing at the prisoner.

"Yes, well done. At least it proves that you can read as well!" replied Jack, still enjoying the moment.

"Well the question that I want the answer to is a simple one. Would kindly tell me just how long were originally you sent down for?" said Dave with a blank expression on his face.

The prisoner stopped smirking and stared at Dave and the governor with his head now on the side. Wondering why, if he had read his record did he want to know the answer to that question?

"If you have my record at hand, then you will be able to look that information up yourself!" said Jack, now sounding more cautious than cocky this time.

"Oh, go on, why don't you just humour me, after all you can't be accused of being a grass when you are only talking about your own length of sentence, can you? So go on, just for saying sake!" said Dave looking straight at him.

"Seven years is what the judge said when he sent me down, why?" said Jack now beginning to fidget about on his chair.

Dave, as soon as he got the reply from the prisoner, picked up the prisoner's record printout and looked at it. "Seven years you say?" replied

Dave slowly. "Well according to these records that have only been printed off today by the Governors secretary. You were not sentenced to seven years, in fact now your sentence reads seventeen years, so it looks as though you still have about fifteen more years still left to go!"

"That's a fucking lie!" shouted the prisoner standing up and making a dash towards Dave, arms waving about and seething with rage.

In an instant, Dave and the Governor each took a step back as the prisoner officer on duty pressed the alarm bell and then made a grab for the prisoner. Dave watched as the prison officer grabbed the prisoner in what looked like a bear hug and he threw him down onto the ground and then he landed on top of him. That action alone knocked the wind out of him, stopping him from fighting for a few seconds. Then the door the interview room flew open and half a dozen prison officers rushed into the room to help their colleague subdue the prisoner.

"Do you want the prisoner taken down to the segregation block sir?" asked one of the prison officers as they all moved to one side revealing the prisoner trussed up like a turkey using official restraining techniques.

"Have you finished with him?" asked Governor Snow to Dave.

"No! If it is all right with you and if he could be somehow tethered to that fixed table, I would like to continue with our little chat," replied Dave smiling at the agonising position that the prisoners arms and body was in.

The Governor nodded to his staff and they then used a pair of handcuffs and secured the prisoner to the table leg, and sat him down again. For safety reasons three prison officers remained in the room while the interview commenced.

"Right then Mr Wilkinson," said Dave in his authorative sounding voice. "As you can see for yourself, the term that you are marked down here for is as I told you before, seventeen years," as Dave placed the copy of that part of his record on the table in front of him.

"But that can't be right?" shouted Jack banging his head onto the table. "You've fixed it just to make me talk, you bastard!"

"Look Wilkinson," said the Governor. "This man does not have any access to your records. As you already now, these are kept solely on the Prison Service secure website and can only be accessed by people that have the correct passwords. My secretary had to download these for the DCI to look at when he arrived."

"It would appear that this Ferris character has tried to screw all of us," said Dave moving closer to the prisoner. "I can, in a way understand him trying to screw the police up and even the prison service. However, to do this sort of thing to the very person that had helped him to achieve these things, is the lowest of low in my book. So you tell me why you still think that you owe him all this bull shit loyalty?"

The room fell silent as jack Wilkinson just sat there with his head now resting on the table in front of him. "Ok copper, what is it that you want to know?"

"Right first of all, did Ferris tell you what he intended to do when he got out?" asked Dave calmly.

"Look, all he told me was that he intended to make the coppers that had put him in here suffer for what they had done to him!" said Jack quietly. "But as far as to what he actually had planned, he never told me anything about that. I don't suppose that he thought that he could completely trust me!"

"I have a feeling that you are right seeing as though he had managed to hack into the prison system and arrange his own release and at the same time make sure that you were not going to get out for a lot longer also!" said Dave now realising the irony of all this.

"Ok Governor, I think that there is nothing more to be learnt here from this person so I think he can be removed," said Dave moving to one side.

As the prison, officers released the prisoners, handcuffs and reapplied the wrist restraints. He suddenly called out to the Governor," They will change the date of my release back to what it should be, won't they?"

The Governor looked at Dave and then to the prisoner and replied, "Well, I will see what I can do but there are no promises!"

"You bastard, after all this!" shouted Wilkinson as he was frogmarched out of the room.

"Was that snippet of information any good for you?" asked Governor Snow.

"Yes it was," replied Dave. "At least now I have had it confirmed that Ferris was intending to take his revenge on both my partner and me for his incarceration."

Outside the prison in the car park, Dave stopped and took a deep breath of fresh air and only then did he realise how dank the air smelt inside that place. Tom saw him approaching the car and got out.

"Is everything ok sir?" asked Tom, who was looking and feeling much better inside.

"Yes Tom, everything is finally beginning to fall into place for the very first time," said Dave getting into the car. "Now let's all go back home, shall we?"

Tom set off, and straightaway Dave could see that the tension from earlier on in the day had somehow dissolved and been lifted off Tom.

"How are you feeling now Tom after that long drive?" asked Dave smiling.

"I don't know what it is sir but all of a sudden I feel like my old self again, maybe, it's the Island?" replied Tom looking and obviously feeling very relaxed.

"Ah, you could have a point there after all!" said Dave as he settled back into his seat.

15

It was daylight, when Bill awoke after feeling refreshed for the first time since this nightmare began. The fire though had long gone out, and the temperature inside the wooden hut was cold enough for Bill to see his own breath. Walking over to where the door was, Bill peeped through one of the many gaps that were in the door surround. Outside there was a thin coating of snow lying on the ground just. He took the time to look as far to the left and right of the doorway looking for any signs of wolf footprints in the snow but there were none to be seen.

Now Bill knew that he had two choices. One was that he remains where he was and hope that someone comes by and offer him some assistance. The other option was to leave the shelter of the shack and try to make his own luck by finding a way off this place and locating where the rest of his family is!

Bill looked around the shack looking for some reason for him to stay but he could not find one. So after using some of the old tatty rags that were in the shack as a covering for his feet against the snow and sharp stones, he opened the door and stepped outside. Instantly, the icy wind whipped up all around him making his entire body tremble and shake through the extreme cold.

With one last look at the shack, Bill headed off into the snow. The only thing on his mind was finding his wife and child before it was too late!

As Bill went over the brow of the hill, the wind seemed to pick up speed and he had to start leaning into it just to make any headway. After battling the weather for a while, Bill came to a steep slope that was still covered with a blanket of snow.

"Now do I make my way down there or look for a safer route to take?" though Bill who was now in a quandary as to which direction he should take.

However, before he could make up his mind. Bill's right foot slipped out from beneath him and he began to tumble down the steep slope. Instinctively, Bill tried to roll up into a ball trying to stop himself from becoming injured. Soon the rolling stopped and he found himself sliding down the slope on his back. By now, Bill realised that he was just a passenger on this terrifying journey down to God only know where!

Eventually, the sliding stopped and Bill found himself lying motionless and unable to move after having the wind knocked out of him on the bumpy journey down the hill. When he was able to sit up, Bill carefully checked as much of his body that he could see for any signs of an injury. Luckily, he did not find any signs of blood anywhere but when he tried to stand, he had to drop back down to the ground again after a sharp pain shot though his foot and up his leg.

"What the!" screamed Bill as he grabbed hold of his painful ankle.

A closer examination revealed that he had somehow knocked the ankle on the slide down the hill. Bill untied the scrap of cloth that had been wrapped around his foot for protection and took a handful of snow and packed it between the ankle and the cloth then retied it up again as tight as he could stand. Bill then tried to stand up again although the ankle was still painful the cold from the snow was having a deadening effect on it.

Now mobile again, Bill continued on with his journey. From time to time, Bill would stop and call out hoping that someone near to him would hear his cries and come looking for him. The downside to this plan though was if the pack of wolves were to hear him, would they be inquisitive enough for them to want to come and take a look who was calling, themselves!

Then in the distance, Bill thought that he could see a couple of people walking. Bill stopped and called out to whoever was there, "Hello! Can you hear me?"

"Could this be Roz and Sammy ahead of me?" thought Bill, as he began to almost run towards the couple. "Roz, Sammy I'm behind you!" shouted Bill as the slippery slope suddenly became too much for his feet and he fell flat on his face banging his forehead in the process. The collision must have stunned Bill for a while, because when he came round, there was no sign of the people that had been in front and so close to him anymore.

Now while sitting in the snow with a bump on his head, and the fact that he had also lost sight of the only people that he had seen in ages, threw Bill into a feeling of total despair! This was when he had to finally admit to himself that if his wife and child were alone and also in this sort of place, any hope of them surviving were as slim as his were.

Bill turned his head and looked skywards then shouted out, "God, what have I done to offend you that was so bad, that you've done this to me and my family?"

He then hung his head down low in total disbelief at the position that he now found himself in. Then from nowhere, Bill's frustration and disbelief began to change to anger and bloody mindedness. It was then that he struggled to his feet, held his fist up in the air and shouted aloud.

"Well fuck you all. Neither my family nor I asked for this crap and I'm surely not fucking ready to give in to you. So I'll do you a deal, you let my family go home safely and you can go and take your best shot at me, how about that?"

Without waiting for any reply no matter how futile, that seemed. Bill now felt pumped up and headed off into the unknown. After about another hour of gruelling trudging through the snow and cold a shape of a small building could just be made out by Bill in the distance. Inspired by what he had seen, Bill headed straight towards it. Eventually Bill was close enough to see that it was yet another wooden shack. "Bloody hell, they must grow these things around here," said Bill looking for any signs of life.

"Look, there are footprints on the ground!" said Bill aloud. This encouraged him to move more quickly towards the shack and possible safety. Standing at the door, Bill took a breath and knocked hard on the wood but there was no reply. So he decided to try the latch on the door to see if it would open.

Click! The door was unlocked and Bill slowly pushed it open. "I don't fucking believe it?" shouted Bill at the top of his voice. "This is the same fucking shack that I left hours ago, but how is that possible?"

Bill stepped inside the shack and closed the door behind him. Sitting on the tatty ram shackled bed, Bill tried to make some sense of all this. "How can you leave a place and fall half way down the side of a fucking mountain and still end up back exactly where you started from!"

It was then that a combination of exhaustion and disbelief fell across Bill like a heavy blanket and he uncontrollably drifted off into a deep sleep!

———————

16

At the Yard, Dave was still trying to work out what Ferris had in mind for Bill and he, when the phone rang out breaking Dave's concentration.

"Hello, yes this is he," said Dave.

Dave listened to what the caller had to say then replied, "Oh Christ, that's all we need right now!" as he replaced the phone back onto its cradle.

Dave then thought for a minute then picked up the phone again and made contact with the police control room. "Hello, this DCI Geraint. I urgently need police back up at the following address and you ought to have an armed response unit close by as well!" Dave then gave the address and the name of the people that lived there. "Oh will you also tell my driver to be downstairs a.s.a.p."

Downstairs, Tom was waiting in the police car with the engine already running. As Dave got into the car Tom said, "I believe that I know where we are going too. I had a quick word with my mate who also works in the control room."

"Good," replied Dave almost sounding a little impressed with Tom's initiative. "So then what are you waiting for?"

With that, Tom drove out of the rear of Scotland Yard as soon as he was on the main road. On went the blues and two's, telling everyone ahead of them to get out of the way and quickly. Tom was in his element once more, driving at high speed and cutting through the traffic like a well-choreographed dance.

As they drew closer to their goal, Dave told Tom to slow down and to turn off the lights and sirens. At a pre-arranged, place a couple of streets away from the address, Dave met up with the support group that by now also included the armed police.

"When Tom and I make entry to the address on our own. I want the rest of you to take up positions very close by but not where you can be seen from the property. If, however they try to leave, you must prevent that from happening otherwise we could have a bloodbath on our hands in London. My job is to go inside there and try to calm the situation down before it can escalate into a full on underworld war!" said Dave to the group. "Are there any questions?"

Dave looked around the group of experienced coppers and knew that he and Tom would be in safe hands if things went wrong!

As Dave and Tom drew up outside the front gates, Tom looked and felt very nervous. "What do you want me to do when we get in there?" asked Tom quietly.

Dave could see the tension that was now on Tom's face and replied, "Nothing at all. Your job is to remain inside the car no matter what happens. You will know if there is a problem when you see the backup team baying at the front gates. When they reach here, then and only then are you to get out of the car and follow the leader's instructions to the letter. Do you understand?"

"Yes sir!" replied Tom looking a little better.

At the gate, Dave got out of the car then went around to the gates intercom and pressed the button. "Yes, who is it?" said a male voice in a curt manner.

"This is DCI Geraint from Scotland Yard and I would like to see a Mrs Sonya Peterson."

"I'm sorry but she is not able to see you at this moment in time," replied the man's voice in an instant.

"Ok then can you tell me if Frankie is there and if he is then I believe that it would be in his interests for him to speak to me!" said Dave in his authorative sounding voice.

The intercom fell silent and Dave turned and looked towards Tom and gave him a sly wink. Then without any further communication, the front gates began to open. Dave jumped back in the car and Tom drove him up the drive to the front door of the house.

At the door there were two huge men standing there waiting for them to arrive. "Now remember what I told you Tom and whatever happens you do nothing until the cavalry arrive, ok!" said Dave as he opened the car door.

"Thank you gentlemen, I must take from this that Frankie is here after all!" said Dave as the two men parted allowing him to enter the now open front door.

Tom watched nervously as Dave walked ahead of the men and the front door closed behind them. Now both Dave and he were, on their own and Tom wondered what was going to happen next?

Inside the house, Dave was directed through to a large room where there were several men standing about. As he entered the room, everyone stopped talking and turned to look at him. Dave Stopped for a second looking for the face of either Frankie or Sonya.

"So why are you here?" said a male voice coming from behind the group of men.

Dave took a deep breath and began to walk towards the sound of the man's voice. As he did so the other men that were there, moved to one side allowing Dave to through. The atmosphere that was in the room was electric, Dave recognised some of the faces present and he knew from past experience, that these were not nice people to have around you. Especially as he was now walking inside the lion's den, so to speak!

Finally, Dave came face to face with Frankie who was sitting on the edge of a large desk. "Well copper, what do you want this time? As you can see, I am rather busy at the moment!"

Dave casually looked around at the faces of the men stood close to him and replied, "Mmm, yes

I can see that, are you having a party or something like that?"

Dave's little quip fell on deaf ears and actually managed to piss a couple of the men there off.

"What do you mean barging your way in here!" someone shouted out from the back of the room.

"Ok lads, why don't we see what this ballsy copper has to say to us before we go any further," said Frankie holding up his hands and indicating to the others to quieten down. "Right then copper, you have five minutes and then I will have to ask you to leave as we have business somewhere else and it can't wait!"

"Well first things first, replied Dave moving so that he had some space around him. "I already am aware where you are going to and I am here to try to prevent that from happening."

"On your own, you've got some fucking hope!" came, a shout from the rear of the group.

Frankie rubbed his chin and then smiled, "Ah, but I have a feeling that you haven't come here on your own, have you copper?"

"Right first time!" replied Dave, much to the dislike of the other men around him. "Look, why don't you hear what I have come here to say and then we will take things from there, ok!"

The room fell silent as Frankie eyed up this ballsy copper standing in front of him and wondered what it was that he had to say. "Ok, I will listen to what you have to say but if I don't like it then you had better have a lot of coppers out there if you think that you are going to stop us from leaving here!"

"Fair enough," said Dave. "Right first of all I now know who was responsible for your brother's death and I can tell you categorically that it had nothing to do with the Dyer family."

"Oh, you would say that if only to stop there from being a war between us!" Shouted out someone, from behind Dave.

"Yes you are correct when you say that I am here to try and prevent a battle ground occurring on the streets of London. But if you are going to start a battle just on the basis of false information then you are not as clever as I had given you credit for," said Dave standing up straight and facing the men.

"Well if you say that you know who killed him then why don't you tell us then?" said Frankie scowling at Dave.

"His name was Norman Ferris. He made good his escape from Parkhurst prison on the Isle of Wight a few months ago. His intended victims were my Sergeant and I for preventing him from blowing up a plane bound for Australia that had his wife and child on board. You see the other week, I was on holiday down in Cornwall and unbeknown to me, he had tried to shoot me three times. Either he must have been a terrible shot or he just meant to kill those three people that had been standing close to me at some time. The weapon that he used was a special gun that used gas cartridges to propel a deadly missile towards its intended target. This resulted in there being no sound coming from the weapon concerned. I personally believe that he had no idea who he was shooting at. Because the other two victims, a man and a young woman both lived in the town where they were killed. In fact, your brother was the only victim that did not live locally."

"Ok, so you say that this chap Ferris intended to kill you. So where is he now?" asked Frankie to the nods of agreement from the others.

"Dead," replied Dave, which resulted in a gasp coming from some of the men standing there.

"That's handy, you have come to tell us that a dead man was responsible for Jamie's death and conveniently he is now dead! What do you think we are Idiots!" said Frankie standing up and trying to excite the men around him.

"Look, the only reason that he is dead, is due to the fact that my driver and I had to run him over in our police car to prevent him from killing again," said Dave.

"And where did all this happen?" asked Frankie, not sounding very convinced with the DCI's story.

"Opposite the DOG & Duck pub," replied Dave instantly.

"Hang on a minute," said one of the men. "I remember that happening. Didn't he get knocked through a plate glass window and die there of his injuries?"

"Yes, I'm sorry to say," said Dave leaning against the desk. "So you see the Dyer family this time had nothing to do with the death of Jamie. He like the others was, just in the wrong place at the wrong time. I can understand how distressing all this can be but you can't bring him back just by blaming the wrong person for his death!"

Frankie then left the room and Dave was left there on his own. He could feel everyone's eyes glaring at him and he knew that anyone of them would not be sorry if any harm was to somehow befall him. Then the door to the room opened and through it came Frankie, who was this time accompanied by Sonya, Jamie's widow.

"Ok lads would you give us a few minutes," said Frankie to the men that had been standing around.

The room quickly emptied leaving only the three of them in there. "I would like you to tell Sonya here, what you have just told me and the lads about who killed Jamie," said Frankie as he sat next to Sonya on a sofa.

Dave then repeated his story about Norman Ferris and awaited the outcome.

"Are you sure, that, that person was responsible for my husband's death in the way that you have just said?" said Sonya looking deep into Dave face.

Dave leaned forward so that his face was directly in front of hers and said, "Yes, one hundred percent sure."

Frankie and Sonya then went into a huddle and soon after she said to Dave, "I have just told

Frankie that I believe what you have just told us about how and even more critically by whom, Jamie was killed. I can tell you now that there will not be any repercussions taken against the Dyer family for Jamie's death. I would also like to say that there are not many police officers that would have come in here like the way you have, to try to explain the situation in the way that you did, so for that I thank you!"

"No, I must thank you for seeing reason amongst all of this chaos," said Dave standing up. "Now I believe that it is time that I took my leave and let you get on with your grieving at this most trying time."

Frankie stood up and walked with Dave to the front door. "I must say that you have got some balls coming here like you did!"

Yes, and more importantly, I'm actually leaving here with them still intact!" replied Dave as he thanked Frankie for listening and returned to the police car.

"Let's get out of here Tom before they decide to change their minds shall we!" said Dave giving out a huge sigh of relief.

As the y cleared the front gates, Dave got on the police radio and instructed the backup team to stand down and thanked them for being there just in case.

"Where to now?" asked Tom.

"The Yard please, Tom and this time there is no hurry!" replied Dave.

———————

17

Something happened to make Bill suddenly wake up with a start. As he opened his eyes, the first thing that he saw, was the white cloud of breath in front of him. "Oh hell, have the wolves found me again?" thought Bill, as he lay there motionless.

It was while he was lying there that the reality of the situation finally dawned on him. What he was looking at was the exhaled breath that was coming from him. The cloud like appearance was from where the warm air from inside his body met with the icy cold atmosphere inside the shack. With the thoughts of ravenous wolves fading into the background, Bill tried to draw himself up into a sitting position. This proved to be far more of an effort than he had experienced before. Then his body began to shake uncontrollably. It began in his chest and then rapidly spread out to the extremities.

"Bloody hell it's freezing in here!" thought Bill as he tried once again in vain to stand up.

Tentatively he reached out and pulled whatever bits of old rag that he could reach towards him. Then with shaking hands, he tried to use the scraps of cloth to cover his extremities. When this seemed to be having very little effect as far as warming him, up. He then attempted to make up a make shift cover that stretched between his knees and the top of his head. Using some small pieces of cloth, Bill attempted to block the sides on either side of his knees. When he could do no more, Bill began to exhale his warm breath into the enclosed space between his chest and his knees. At first, he could not feel anything. Then very slowly, a tingle of warmth could be felt entering the pores of the skin and slowly penetrating further into his body. This effort though was very exhausting and as soon as he felt able, Bill made an extreme effort to stand up and move about.

"Somehow I've got to try and light that fire again, if there is going to be any chance of me surviving this ordeal!" thought Bill as he looked around for something to burn.

Apart from the walls of the wooden shack, the only wooden item left that would burn was the bed. So using every ounce of strength that he had left in his body, Bill began to break up the bed and its frame ready for burning. After gathering up the smaller pieces and putting them on the bottom of the wood burner. Bill then looked around for some cobwebs to place on top hoping that they would catch fire, as they had the last time. However, try as he might, there were no more cobwebs to be found.

"I wonder if dust will burn?" thought Bill moving across to the tatty shelves and scooping a pile of what looked like decades old particles of dust and gently placing it on top of the kindling. "Now where did I put those two bits of flint that I used before?"

Bill searched the shack high and low looking for the only two things that would make a spark to enable him to light the fire and warm up! This searching though took its toll on Bill and after a fruitless search; he dropped onto the wooden floor totally, disillusioned. With his head lying heavy in his hands, Bill began to shake his head wondering what else could go wrong!

It while his mind was still reeling from the feeling of despair that through his fingers, he suddenly noticed the two pieces of flint. For some reason, they were lying on the floor beneath the wood burner. Seeing them raised Bill expectations as he reached out and picked them up. Then rubbing them together, Bill tried to get them to produce a spark. This was not going to be easy due to the fact, that by now his body temperature had rapidly dropped making his hands shake. This would assist him in striking the stones together if only he could control their actions enough!

He then moved closer to the opening of the wood burner and tried to wedge his one hand against the side of the container. Then he used his free hand to try to strike the two flint stones together. Eventually a spark could be seen, almost jumping from the stone in slow motion and onto the shallow pile of ancient dust. Bill watched as the smouldering ember made contact with the dust. At first, it appeared to glow when it first made contact, then s Bill watched it began to fade as it sank out of sight beneath the dust's surface.

"Oh come on, at least give me a bloody fighting chance!" shouted Bill at the open doorway to the burner.

Now whether it was luck, or the air from Bill's shout for help, as he watched, a small wisp of smoke began to rise up from the pile of dust. This time though, Bill held his breathe, as he was almost transfixed watching the wisp of smoke grow bigger and bigger until finally Bill could see a flicker of light coming from the kindling below. Gingerly, Bill added extra bits of wood to the now flaming fire until finally he could place a much larger piece on and finally close the door and sit back on the floor and take in the warmth.

As his body began to warm up, Bill went and filled the tin can as before with snow from outside and placed it on top of the wood burner to get a hot drink. With heat to his once cold body and sipping a hot drink, thoughts once again turned to the fate of his wife Rosalynd and their son Sammy. The feeling of hopelessness was overwhelming and the tears began to roll down Bills face when he thought of what they must be going through. There only interruption was from the rumbles that were coming from his now very empty stomach. Since his ordeal had begun, not one morsel of food had passed his lips and it was now having an effect on Bills strength levels. At least though for now, he could get some nourishment from the hot watery drink that he had made out of the melted snow.

Through all of this, one nagging question still remained in Bill's mind, and that was, why is all of this happening to him and his family?

He knew in his heart that these questions were never going to be answered while he remained trapped where he was. How to escape though now seemed to be beyond his ability. First, of all, he had no idea where he was or in which direction he had to go to have a chance of getting out of here! Then there was the fact of his diminishing levels of strength. He soon would have to make the decision as to whether to try to make his escape and risk freezing out in the open if he was to fail. On the other hand, he could stay where he is until the wood runs out, and then freeze!

"Well it looks like I have got one hell of a list of options here," said Bill aloud to himself. "Let's see, I must soon decide to either die here or die out there. What a choice for a person to make?"

Then for the first time, Bill's thoughts drifted to his old pal Dave. "I wonder if he even knows that my family and I are all missing yet?" thought Bill. "If Dave is aware, then I am sure that he will somehow manage to find us and bring us back home again. I only hope that it is sooner than later, otherwise I might have to resort to a third option and that is not one that appeals to me!"

18

In his office, Dave found a scrap of paper telling him to go to the forensic department a.s.a.p.

"Well, I wonder what snippet of information they have managed to find now?" thought Dave to himself as he left his office.

As Dave entered the forensic lab, Billy one of their resident techno freaks greeted him. "Hello Dave I'm glad to see that you have the time to come down here and rough it from time to time!"

"Yeh, yeh, so what have you found that has got you so excited?" said Dave, knowing only too well that when Billy starts to explain things normally, he is hard to understand. However, when he is this excited, it's, as though he suddenly starts speaking a foreign language, as far as he is concerned.

"Well, it's like this?" said Billy, "It appears that somehow an electronic byte or device has been developed and sent to you!"

"Fucking hell Billy, have you completely forgotten how to speak in English?" said Dave shaking his head. "Look, for once, will you say what you have to say slowly and by using words that even mortals have a chance of understanding!"

Billy then stopped what he was doing and looked as though he was having to re-boot his mind down to a normal level of understanding.

"Ok, look, ah I've got it!" said Billy standing up. "Have you got your mobile phone on you?"

Dave felt his pockets and then replied, "Yes, why?"

"Right, here is the number of this department," said Billy all excited. "What I want you to do, is to ring that number and then see what happens next!"

By now, Dave was at a point where he thought that it was easier to go ahead with Billy's ideas than to try to reason with him!

Dave entered the phone number into his phone and then pressed the send button. At first, there was the usual delay as the mobile system sorted out which phone to ring. Then virtually on cue, the telephone on the desk began to ring out. Dave, who was by now looking really impressed at the power of his phone just shrugged his shoulders and said half-heartedly, "Well, what has that proved?"

"Just you wait a few seconds and you will see!" replied Billy eagerly rubbing his hands together.

As Dave watched Billy's impression of a mad scientist at work, a mobile phone that was sitting on the table next to where Billy was standing suddenly began to vibrate and then ring out.

"Do you see that?" said Billy all excited.

"Yes, that's very clever," replied Dave politely not really understanding, what the hell Billy was actually talking about.

"Look, you said that you could not understand how that man always seemed to know where you were at any time. What he had done at some time was to send you a text message that had a type of relay device implanted inside it. Then whenever you used your mobile to arrange to go anywhere, all he had to do was to track you using the now built in homing device. He may not have known where you were actually going to but he was able to locate your position down to a few feet!" explained Billy smiling from ear to ear.

"Are you positive about this?" asked Dave who had now formed a new opinion of Billy.

"100% sure!" replied Billy as he spun round and round on his chair.

"Well I'm blowed!" said Dave. "And here I was beginning to think that there was something weird going on, when all the time it had been me that had been telling him where to find me. I will need you to bag all of this kit up as evidence and then make a report about this for my boss. But, first of all can you disable that homer for me? Just in case there is another person out there who is still in a position to listen!"

Dave then handed over his mobile to Billy who took it away into another room. Then a few minutes later returned and handed it back to Dave.

"You've done as quick, as that?" asked Dave.

"Yes, if you don't believe me then try that number that I gave you earlier and see what happens?" replied Billy sitting down again.

So Dave retyped in the number and then pressed the send button. Seconds later the office phone began to ring out.

"See!" said Billy smiling.

Dave waited to see if the other phone rang but nothing happened. Then he moved across to where Billy was sitting and picked up his mobile and checked to see if it was still switched on, and it was!

"Boy, you don't trust anyone do you!" said Billy as Dave handed his phone back to him.

"In words of one syllable, the answer to that question is NO!"

Dave then thanked Billy for all his help, before returning to his office.

———

19

Dave then called a meeting of some of his colleagues in the office and went over what they now knew about Norman Ferris. Dave was now in a position to bring them up to date with all that he discovered when he had come across him previously at Heathrow Airport. That time, his intentions were to bring down a plane that had on board his wife and child. He had devised a plan to cripple the plane in such a way that if successful, it would look as though the crash had been either through mechanical failure or put down to pilot error!

He then told them what Billy down in the Forensic department had discovered. This brought many shakes of the heads from those around Dave. Now they realised that this person, although disturbed was also very clever at creating things to achieve his goals!

"Did I hear that a front door key had been found on the body?" asked one of the people.

"Yes, you are correct," replied Dave. "Unfortunately for us, we have no idea as to what name he has been using or even an area for us to begin looking!"

The room fell silent as many minds chewed over what they had just heard. Then out of the silence, someone asked, "You mentioned that he had a mobile phone, is that right?"

"Yes, but it was broken when he fell to the floor after being shot!" replied Dave. "Why do you ask?"

"Well, if we could discover from the phones supplier where most of his calls had been made from. Using a triangulation method taken from the various mobile masts that are situated all around the Capital. We might, if we are lucky be able to shorten the area down to only a few metres!"

"Well done!" said Dave as a ripple of applause rang out from the other people there. "Your name is Tony isn't it?"

"Yes sir, Tony Davies."

"Well Tony Davies, what I think your next move should be is for you to take yourself along to the forensic department and have a word with Billy. Tell him your theory and then maybe between the pair of you the past negative information will be able to change to a positive one. So go on and let me know if you have any success!" said Dave looking rather impressed with the young man's attitude.

While Tony headed off. Dave brought the other members of the team up to date about the disappearance of Bill and his wife and son.

"The fact that Ferris had mentioned Bill when he was aiming his gun at me has put a very different slant onto looking for them. Until

Ferris mentioned them, I just thought that they had gone off somewhere without telling me. Now that I am aware that they haven't and that Ferris has had something to do with it now has me very concerned about their safety. What I want is for two of you to go along to Bill's home and look for an address book or telephone notebook. Then you will have to try to make contact and ask if any of them have seen or heard from them over the past few days. But whoever does the calling, please be diplomatic and choose your questions with sensitivity. What we do not want are their relatives coming down here offering to help look for them!" said Dave. "The rest of you will need to go back over all of the paperwork and look for anything that might have been overlooked!"

With that, the people split up into smaller groups and went off with the intention of locating one of their own before another life was chalked up to that man, Ferris!

20

Almost hypnotised by the flickering flames from the wood burner in front of him, Bill's mind was at present far away from this nightmarish place. He was remembering playing in the park on a hot summer's day with his wife Rosalynd and son Sammy. How happy they had been playing on the swings and eating ice cream. Bill also wondered about his old friend Dave, where was he? Was he looking for them or had he found himself in a similar hellhole as Bill's was!

If he was missing too, was anyone looking for them and more important, would they manage to find them in time!

As Bill's mind jumped from one subject to another, a strange sound suddenly brought him back to his own reality. Jumping up, Bill looked around him to see what the noise had been. At first, he could see nothing untoward but then his eyes were drawn back to the wood burner. There he soon discovered that the sound he had heard was that of the burnt pieces of wood falling onto the grill.

"Oh shit, the fire is almost out!" said Bill aloud.

He looked around the shack for more bits of wood to burn. Since he had been there, he had virtually stripped the shack of all things that could be burnt. The only wood that remained was the floor walls and roof. Bill decided to begin pulling up some of the floorboards and breaking them up and feeding them into the burner trying not to douse the now fickle flames. Now Bill found that he had another problem and that was where he had removed the flooring, icy blasts of cold air was now entering the shack through the gaps. This then meant that he needed to take more planks up just to produce enough heat to prevent himself from freezing.

Bill was now in a desperate situation. He knew in his heart that once the flooring had all gone, then he would die through the extreme cold once the fire went out. He sat down close to the wood burner and tried to keep out of the ever-present blasts of cold air.

"This is a God forsaken place," thought Bill as he watched the flames get stronger as the fire took a hold of the wood and began devouring it. As he watched almost mesmerised at the flames flickering like dancers on a stage, his attention was quickly drawn to another sound, and this one was coming from the front door! Slowly and without trying to make a sound, Bill stood up and moved quietly towards the front door, then placed his ear to the door and listened. What he heard was a strange snuffling sort of noise that he had never heard before and it put Bill in a quandary. Should he open the door and see what was making the strange sound, or does he look through the dirty old window?

His experience as a copper held him in good stead and he quickly realised that caution was the best path to choose, in this now deadly game. So after quietly edging his way from the door to the side window, Bill slowly moved his head in front of the dirty pane of glass and looked outside. Now from this position, he was not able to see what was waiting on the other side of the front door, if he was to have opened it. Even though he craned his head looking towards the door trying to glimpse a shadow or something, he remained unsighted. Then as he stood at the window, the strange snuffling noise suddenly stopped. Now there was an eerie silence and Bill's mind began to race with all different permutations as to what would happen next!

After waiting for a few seconds, listening to see if the strange sound started up again, Bill moved back to the side window for another look outside. At first, there were no signs of anything moving about outside. Then, as he turned his head to look the other way he saw the huge head of a grey coloured wolf leaping up towards him.

Bang!

The huge wolf hit the pane of glass directly in front of Bill's face. In a flash, Bill could see the rows of sharp teeth that had globules of white saliva dripping off them. Although where the wolf had hit the pane of glass somehow did not break it! The shock of seeing the wolf jumping up at him and the rattle of the wooden wall as the wolf's paws banged hard against it, made Bill instinctively hurl himself back away from the window. Unfortunately, as he did so, he tripped over one of the gaps in the floor and fell back against the wood burner, knocking it over in the process. This sudden jolt spilled the contents of the burner out onto the floor of the shack. When the burning wood dropped onto the floor, its door flew open meeting up with the icy blast of cold air coming through the floor. This had the disastrous effect of almost immediately extinguishing, what tenuous flame there was, resulting in the rapid loss of heat.

Bill tried to blow onto the charred pieces of wood with the hope that he could rekindle a spark or two of flames once more. But he soon realised that his attempts were hopeless. So now with at least one hungry wolf prowling about outside and the loss of his only heat source, Bill's world once more dropped into a deep abyss of despair!

He now realised for the first time that he was never going to be able to escape from this terrible place alive. At present, there were now only two thoughts etched on Bill's mind. They were how was the end going to finally come, would it be through the cold and freeze to death, or from the wolf and that was as far as his mind could take!

———————

21

The telephone rang out on DCI Geraint's desk and he reached across to pick it up. "Hello, yes this is he. Are you sure of that?" said Dave becoming all excited. Replacing the phone Dave called to the other members of his team to update them with the latest news.

"I have just heard from Tony and he tells me that the techno people have managed to narrow the search area for where Ferris used to live. From all accounts, the signal from his mobile has pinpointed an area to the right hand side of the DOG & DUCK pub where we last saw him. So they suggest that house to house enquiries should be made in the old quarter rather than in the newly built places that are around there."

"Why there?" asked one of the team.

"Well if he were staying in the new area, then he would have to show documentation to prove who he really was. However, in the old area, that sort of thing is not usually needed as they don't always tell the authority about letting out rooms, in case it should draw any unwanted attention from them!" replied Dave. "So what I need you to arrange is for the local bobby's to have two copies of our man. One with his beard and the other without, that way at least we might get lucky and someone might decide to tell us the truth about seeing him. Please stress that we are not interested whether they are letting room illegally or not, the priority is for us to locate this man's home. Until we can achieve that, then we will not get any closer to finding Bill or his family!"

With that, people began moving about organising ready for the search to begin.

"Dave!" called someone from the other side of the office. "I have someone on the line asking to speak to you."

"Who is it?" asked Dave still scanning through the piles of paperwork in front of him.

"She says that her name is Rosalynd or something like that!"

Dave stood up so quick that his chair was thrown backwards against the office wall. He rushed across the phone and snatched out of the man's hand.

"Rosalynd is that you? Are you, Bill and little Sammy alright?" said Dave almost stammering his words down the telephone.

"Hello Dave, yes this is Rosalynd. Why are you asking if we are all safe? I don't understand, Bill should have told you that Sammy and I had been up here to visit with my parents in Bolton for a few days," said Rosalynd in a concerned tone of voice. "And why did you ask me if Bill was with me, is he ok?"

"But we tried to make contact with your family but were unsuccessful!" replied Dave, his head now in a total spin from receiving this wonderful phone call.

"Oh the reason for that is due to the fact that they have only recently moved to another place in Bolton and that is why me and Sammy have come up here to have a look at it!" replied Rosalynd.

With a partial relief, Dave then tried his best to explain what had happened down here while she and her son had been away. When Dave began to explain about Bill being missing that was when Rosalynd began to get into a panic on the phone.

"Look Dave, I'm coming straight down to London on the first available train. If my Bill is missing, then he will want both Sammy and me to be there when he is found!" said Rosalynd in a sobbing voice.

"No! You must not come back here yet," snapped Dave in a loud voice. "If you and Sammy come down here then you could be putting both of your lives in danger, and Bill for one would not thank me for allowing that to happen. I need for you to remain where you are and I will keep you informed of any progress that is made with regards to finding Bill, ok!"

"But if the man who you say is responsible for my Bill's disappearance is now dead, why would there still be a threat to us?" said Rosalynd, her voice now sounding more composed.

"That is because we are not sure that this person was working alone. If he did have a partner, then after Ferris's death the other person could take their revenge out on you or that of your son Sammy!" said Dave, hoping against hope that he had convinced her not to come back here to London.

There was a long pause, before Rosalynd replied. "If you promise to keep me informed of any progress and think that it would be for the best, then we will stay up here," said Rosalynd in a reluctant voice. "But I will not wait up here forever, you understand!"

"I promise," replied Dave feeling relieved that at least they were safe from harm where they were. "And thank you for being so understanding!"

Dave hung up the phone and he began to well up with emotion. Partly because he now knew that Rosalynd and Sammy were both safe, but now he began to feel under even more pressure to locate where Bill was and get him back safely to his loving family.

"Who was that?" someone asked bringing Dave back down to reality.

"That was Bill's wife Rosalynd," said Dave, feeling happier inside than he had for a long time. "From all accounts, she and their son Sammy have been up in Bolton visiting their recently moved parents and that was why we could not make contact with them earlier on"

Dave then made sure that he notified the other members of his team about the good news, concerning Bill's family. Now they now could concentrate all of their efforts in finding their colleague Bill, wherever he was.

22

The area of London that had been indicated by the techno boys back at the Yard as a prime target. This area was consequentially flooded with police officers as well as special constables. Each pair had with them pictures of their man Norman Ferris. Hours went by without any positive feedback being received, people either genuinely had no idea who the man Ferris was and the others, just wanted to be obstructive with their reply to the police. Although this was a normal response whenever they had to do these house-to-house enquiries, as it was one of their own that was missing, the frustration seemed to be having a much deeper impact on the officers concerned.

Then from out of the mire of lies and deceit, someone finally recognised the man in the picture. This news was quickly passed onto Dave and the others in the squad.

Within minutes of the call, Dave and a couple of his colleagues were standing outside the address. Looking up at the old building, Dave scanned the windows not really knowing what he was looking for. In front of him stood a three storey, building that had been, many years ago converted into bedsits. Dave knew, from past experience that these types of places were usually frequented by what they normally called, the transient population. This meant that they usually knew none of the other people that frequented the property due to the fact that they never stayed there that long.

Entering the property through the front door, the team were met with a rank smell that permeated through the entire building. Next, was the rubbish that was strewn across the floor making it difficult to walk unimpeded?

"What d'you lot want then?" said a scruffy looking man as he stepped through the doorway opposite.

"Well I hope so," said Dave politely. "I am DCI Geraint and these people here with me are members of my team. We have been informed that this person lives here!"

Dave then took out the picture of Ferris and showed it to the man. At first, the man seemed reluctant to look at the picture, but when Dave explained to him that they were not there from the housing people, he seemed relieved and nodded his head. "Yes he lives here," said the man. "Top floor number nine, but he ain't there at the moment!"

"Number nine you say?" said Dave as he headed up the stairs with the other members of the team following close behind.

The further up the stairs they went, the stronger the stench became. On the second floor, they passed what appeared to be the bathroom and toilet. A man opened the door and the acrid smell made a couple of them wrench as they took an unwanted whiff of the aromatic aroma that filled the entire landing. Finally, they stood outside number nine. "Do we knock and wait to see if anyone answers or do we just go in?" someone asked.

With that, Dave lifted up his right foot and promptly kicked in the door. As the door flew open it slammed into the wall behind making a loud bang. This brought a couple of the other residents to their doorways to have a look at what was happening. "What the fucks going on here?" one of the men shouted out in an angry voice.

"It's the police, so for your own safety we advise that you return back into your own rooms and leave us to get on with our business!" called out one of Dave's team

This had the desired effect and soon door were slamming closed all around them. It was quite obvious that the last thing that these people wanted was a brush with the law.

Inside room nine was a one-room bedsit, that could only be described as being a shitty hovel. The net curtains instead of being a brilliant white colour were in fact a dirty brown, tainted after years of people smoking in the room. The single bed had sheets on it, but nobody in the room wanted to touch it never mind search it. In fact, the place was so disgustingly filthy, some of the team put on extra pairs of rubber gloves just in case they were to get a hole in them. After an hour of searching the room, they all left there disillusioned that they had not found a single thing that could point them in the direction to find Bill.

On the trip back to the Yard, several of the team said that they needed to take a shower after being in that place. "I don't know how on earth, any human being can live, in a place like that?" one of them said.

"That's easy," replied Dave. "It's because in those types of places, no-one asked any questions and as far as the authorities are concerned, they don't exist!"

"Well if I had to live like that then I wouldn't want to exist!" came back the reply.

23

In the office, the feeling throughout the team was one of helplessness, their hopes and jubilation at finding where Ferris had lived and the possibility of discovering where Bill was, had now plummeted into the depth of despair. Even though they continued to scour through all of the information that they had accumulated looking for the one thing that might have been overlooked, the room was for now a very quiet place to be.

Feeling as though he could not think straight, Dave stood up and walked out of the office. Downstairs he came across Tom who was for the present assigned to him as a driver. "Take me over to the city morgue will you Tom!" said Dave.

Tom jumped up out of his seat and headed off along the corridor towards the rear car park with Dave following close behind. Dave sat in the back of the police car on the journey to the morgue. Tom could see in his rear view mirror that by the look on the DCI's face, this was not the time for any small talk.

At the morgue, Tom waited with the car and watched as the DCI entered the building.

"Excuse me sir, I'm DCI Geraint and I need to see one of you customers!" asked Dave to one of the officials that were passing by.

The man took a quick look at Dave's ID and then directed him towards a different room further on along a passageway. Entering the room, Dave was then met by one of the pathologists that he knew worked there.

"Hello Dave, what brings you over here?"

"A body, would you believe!" replied Dave sarcastically.

"Well there are quite a few to choose from. Is there anyone in particular that you need to look at?" asked the pathologist smiling.

"Yes, Norman Ferris please," replied Dave straight faced.

"Ok, if you follow me then I will take you to where he is!"

Dave walked behind his guide who took him further into the building far away, from where any of the general public could venture. There he stood in front of a square metal door and Dave watched as he opened it up. Then he reached in and slid the table that had Norman Ferris's body covered on it out so that Dave could take a closer look.

"Would you like me to remain with you?" asked the pathologist politely.

"No, but thank you for asking," replied Dave, as the man quietly left the room leaving Dave alone with the body.

Dave gingerly moved the white cloth away from the corpse's face and took a small step back. "Even in death you have a smug look almost engraved on your ashen face. If you were still alive, then I know a person that has access to a dark place where I could have had great pleasure in discussing your problem with me on a personal basis, but you even managed to cheat me of that little pleasure, didn't you, you, bastard!"

Dave then began to walk up and down the room, searching for the little things that he might have missed. "What have you done with Bill and where is he now?" said Dave aloud. "I already knew that you were a twisted bastard, after you tried to kill your wife and child on the plane. I believe that it was your intention to be killed by the police the other day when you aimed that gun at me. That way, you managed to take where Bill is to your grave with you and for me to suffer like we made you do when we prevented you from committing mass murder!"

Dave then began to walk up and down the room glancing at the body of Ferris each time that he passed by. "You were a clever bastard, pre-planting that homing device in my mobile phone the way that you did. You know it really began to freak my driver out and me, especially when you kept appearing where we were. I started to believe that you were some sort of a ghost, when all it was down to was a simple homing device!"

Dave then stopped and slowly turned towards the body and repeated what he had just said.

"The homing device, that's it!" shouted Dave at the top of his voice.

He then moved closer to where Ferris's body was and said, "Right you bastard, I said that you were clever but this time I do believe that I have managed to even outsmart you!"

Dave's outburst attracted some attention from people that worked there and one of the popped his head around the door and asked, "Is everything alright sir?"

"Yes, perfect!" replied Dave as walked past the man and hurried back to Tom who was still waiting patiently for him. "Tom, back to the Yard and quickly!" shouted Dave at the top of his voice.

As soon as Dave was in the car, Tom switched on the blue lights and the siren then sped off at a high rate of speed back to Scotland Yard. On the way, Dave made contact with Billy in the forensic department and put his ideas to him. Billy promised to try to do what he wanted and would try to have it ready for when Dave got there. The journey through London's traffic was like poetry in motion. Tom judged every distance and gap to perfection and sliced through the normally congested traffic with ease.

Dave had the car door open before it had come to a full stop at the rear of the Yard. He then raced up to the forensic department where he was to be met by some of the other members of his team. Once they were all there, Dave proceeded to try to explain his theory as to how they might be able to locate where Bill was.

"I have just come from standing in front of the body of Norman Ferris at the morgue," said Dave to the sounds of "Ugh" from some of them there.

"Precisely my feelings," replied Dave. "But it was while I was venting my anger, for the want of another word. I remembered how he had been able to track me down by using my mobile. Then it hit me, had he done the same thing to bill's phone and in that way managed to kidnap him! While we speak, Billy is trying to get the device out of the broken phone that Ferris had and seeing if he can make it work in another one. If he can, then maybe, just maybe, we will be able to locate Bill by the homing signal that is being given out by his phone."

"God, I hope that his battery is still charged?" said someone.

"Yes I think that we might need his help to find him this time!" replied Dave as Billy entered the room. "Have you been able to do it?" asked Dave eagerly.

"That I don't know, but I have waited until we were all together before trying it out just in case Bill's battery on his phone is running low," said Billy.

Then with everyone huddled around the table watching closely, Billy switched on the phone!

24

At first, nothing happened and the mood around the table fell flat. Then a faint bleeping sound could just be heard, all eyes the turned and stared at the little screen on the mobile phone. There was an orange dot flashing and bleeping. Behind it was a road map of London and as one of the produced a magnifying glass to enable them to read the name of the road. Another took down the co-ordinates and the name of the road for further information just in case they should lose the signal. As soon as they had achieved that a loud cheer rang out and hugs were the order of the day all round. They now all knew where Bill's mobile was, but was Bill there too, there was only one way to find out and that was to go straight there!

"Well according to these coordinates, the signal from Bill's phone is coming from a position approximately two miles north of the Tower Bridge!" said one of the team, who was looking at the map on his computer.

"Can you tell from that if it is a house or some other building like that?" asked Dave moving across to look at the screen for himself.

"No, not exactly, however from the signals position it would appear that it could be coming from something that is on the river itself!"

"Right then," said Dave grabbing his coat. "We need to get out to this place a.s.a.p. If Bill is there, then time could be of the essence! Will someone make a call and arrange for an ambulance to be standing by in the area just in case medical aid is required if we do locate him."

"I'll do that while you lot head over there!" shouted someone from the back of the room.

Down stairs, police cars were already waiting for them. Dave got into the car being driven by Tom and he gave him the location where they had to get to. With lights flashing and sirens wailing, the convoy of police vehicles roared off from the Yard. On the journey, various scenarios of what he might find went through Dave's head. He knew from past experience that Ferris was no ordinary villain, in the sense that they usually had a single objective, be it, robbery, car theft right up to murder. Ferris never seemed to approach his crimes with any single-minded outcome in mind. On the contrary, he always had to have something that remained hidden and if you were not careful, it would creep up and then bite you in the arse!

"Caution must play its part when we locate the place in question," thought Dave as he watched them pass people as if in a blur. "Otherwise it could result in someone else losing their life and that would be disastrous for all concerned."

As they neared the area indicated by the homing device in Bill's mobile, Dave told Tom to slow down to a crawl until the signal was at its strongest. "It's a bloody good thing that Billy managed to rig up this tracker for u, using another mobile," said Dave staring hard at the screen.

As soon as the single bleeping changed to emit a long bleep, which was when Dave knew that they were very close to their objective. "Right Tom, stop the car here and we will all have to walk the rest of the way!" said Dave as the car drew to a stop.

The road that they were now on ran alongside the River Thames and was just north of the Tower Bridge. Running alongside the pavement was a low wall that had spiked railing mounted into the top. This was so that the view to the river was unimpeded, while preventing anyone from just jumping over and landing in the water far below!

On the other side of the road from the river, were a few old buildings. Some of them were now derelict while others had been modernised into apartments. Dave held out the tracker and began to turn around slowly looking for when the signal was the strongest. He began with the device pointing at the derelict buildings, as they would be the obvious choice to hide someone in. The tracker however told him different and just kept on bleeping. Dave then began to turn to his left and towards the apartment complex but yet again the bleeps remained constant. It was not until he was pointing the device towards the river did the signal rapidly change to a constant tone, indicating that that was the direction that the signal from Bill's watch was coming from. The question now in their, minds was, had someone just thrown Bill's watch into the river. On the other hand, was his body lying in the water below them? The only way to find out was for them all to find a way to get down there and take a look for themselves!

25

Because the view below where they were was partially obstructed by the railings. Immediately, they all split up and looked for a way for them to gain access to that area. It didn't take long before a shout rang out saying, "Over here sir, we have found a way to safely get down!"

Everyone hurried to the gateway that had previously been inset into the railings obviously for access. They all waited until Dave was there and then followed him through the gate that then lead onto a steep path leading down to the side of the riverbank. At the bottom of the slope, they were all confronted with the sight of several barges that were being used as houseboats.

"I had no idea that these were down here!" said from the rear of the team as they reached the bottom of the slope.

"Ok," said Dave, gathering them all into a huddle. "Time could be of the essence here but we must move slowly as there could have been some booby traps laid, just to catch us out. First of all, we need to see if anyone on these barges has ever seen our man and if so, was he ever seen using one of these barges recently!"

The team then broke up into two's and with photos in hand, tried to locate anyone living on the barges. The first two had no one home, the third one however was home and he was able to give the police a positive identification of their man.

"Sir, this gentleman here has recognised Ferris and says that he had seen him go onto the end barge for a short while then he would leave again. He didn't think that he actually lived there as he had never seen him stay there overnight. He did tell me one thing that might or might not be important, and that was that Ferris always seemed to come to the barge at virtually the same time every day and then leave again."

"Now that could be of interest if we find Bill on that barge?" replied Dave as they all made their way along the narrow towpath towards the end barge.

From the towpath, everyone moved quietly trying to see if they could spot anything through the boats side windows. This though was not going to be possible due to the fact that all of the curtains on the barge had been drawn.

"Have a look and see if there is anything attached to the barge, other than the mooring ropes before anyone attempts to get on board just in case he has left any booby traps for us!" said Dave stooping down for a closer look.

After a few seconds stooped down scanning the sides of the barge, Dave stood up and it was only then that he noticed the rest of his team standing about scratching their heads!"

"What's the matter with you lot them?" said Dave, sounding a little pissed off.

"It's just that none of us have any idea what we are looking for? We can see the ropes that are anchoring it to the side but as to whether they should be like that is way out of our expertise!" said one of the men who was still looking at the barge and scratching his head.

Dave for an instance could see the funny side to this and just added, "Well can any of you see any wiring coming from the barge then?"

Seconds later, an echoed response came back shouting out, "No!"

Dave then told the others to stand back while he got on board the barge to take a look around.

"Can I come with you sir?" said a voice from behind Dave.

As Dave turned to see who had spoken just then, he was surprised to see the familiar face of Tom his driver standing behind him. "Ok, if you want to!" replied Dave as he took a long step across from the towpath and onto the barge.

While Dave edged his way to the rear of the barge, he looked back and watched as Tom struggled to make his way along the side of the barge with his size twelve footwear. Then as soon as Tom was standing next to him, Dave tried opening the cabin door unfortunately it had been locked. So Dave looked around for something to use to prize it open. There in front of him, he noticed a crowbar that had been lying on the deck and he picked it up. Then using all of his might, he jammed it into the gap between the door and the outside and then wrenched it back.

———————

26

The cold now was relentless as it forced its way under the shack and through the gaps in the floor. Try as he might, Bill was now losing his battle against the cold and life. Why he was in this awful place was beyond him, his dying thoughts drifted off and he wondered what fate had befell his darling wife Rosalynd and their little boy Sammy. Bill thought about the day when he had been present at Sammy's birth and how proud he was to become a dad for the first time.

As he sat there drifting in and out of consciousness, Bill suddenly became aware of a pulsing sound coming from inside his head. At first, he wondered what it could be, but then when he placed his hand onto his chest, he realised that the pulsing was in the exact rhythm as his own heart. "Is this what happens when you are about to die?" thought Bill to himself. "I suppose that if I listen long enough to the sound, when the beat stops, that's when I die!"

If it was going to be their fate to die, then he felt cheated that he could not be with them at the end. Had all this come about due to something that he had done, or was he and his lovely family just the victims of someone's problematic mind!

Then a loud banging on the door brought Bill back to some sort of reality for the last time. He looked towards the door of the shack and could see the door shake as something on the other side was hitting it trying to get at him.

If this was going to be the end, then let it come quick. That was when the door to the shack suddenly burst open and a dark shadowy figure made a beeline towards him. All Bill could do to defend himself was to raise his hands up in front of him.

As the wooden door flew open, Dave instinctively thrust Tom to one side out of the line of fire, just in case of a trap had been set for them. When nothing happened, Dave and Tom gingerly made their way into the darkened cabin down the narrow wooden steps. Once inside, Dave fumbled around for a light switch. It wasn't long before he found one but for an instant, he wondered once again should he turn it on or not. He realised that he had to turn the light on just in case he missed anything else that could have been set to catch them out!

Click, Dave threw the switch and screwed his eyes up just in case he had made the wrong decision. This time though, only the lights came on. Ahead of them stretched a long narrow passageway that had been divided into sections such as a kitchen and living area. The walls had cupboards situated either side of the small windows that could be used for storage. Slowly they edged their way along the aisle and came face to face with a drawn curtain.

"I bet that this is the bedroom!" said Dave to Tom as he raised his hand up and slid it to one side.

A gasp rang out from both Dave and Tom as their eyes fell onto the body of Bill who was lying on top of the bed motionless. "Tom, go and tell the others what we have found and then get an ambulance down here a.s.a.p.," said Dave as he nervously moved closer to his old friend.

Dave's heart sank at the sight of Bill just lying there motionless, with his arms raised up in front of his now distorted face. That sight of Bill upset Dave dramatically and the tears began to well up inside at the thought of his friend dying in this dire place all alone. As the tears began to fall down his cheeks, Dave, with his head in his hands moved and sat down on the bed next to him. It was then that there came a groan and a sudden movement from Bill's once lifeless body. Dave immediately jumped up off the bed and called out, "He's alive!"

As other members of the team made their way into the barge to see for themselves, euphoria welled up throughout the tight knit group at the sight of their colleague who was still alive.

It was amongst all of this, happiness that Dave then noticed that there were some wires coming from the head of Bill. He decided to trace them and found that they were then, attached to a strange machine that looked just like a black box. "Everybody, hold up a minute!" shouted Dave over the hubbub. "I think that we still could have an explosive problem here so I want you all to leave the barge very quietly, and keep a safe distance away until I can work out what these wires are here for?"

A deathly silence fell across the team as they all made their way off the barge and then collected together away from the barge. "I've made a call to the bomb squad just as a precaution!" said one of them. "They will not however be here for some time, due to other commitments!"

Watching the barge feeling totally, helpless was an agonising feeling for them all. Then down the towpath, came a paramedic carrying his enormous bag of tricks on his shoulder. "Hi guys, what do we have then?" he asked.

He was then quickly brought up to speed with the situation regarding the fate of one of their own men, as they understood it. After listening to what they had to say and with all of that knowledge in mind, to the others surprise, the paramedics just walked off towards the barge.

"We were told to wait here!" shouted one of them, but the paramedic just raised his hand in the air and climbed onto the barge.

The barge moved about when the paramedic clambered on board making Dave wobble about a bit. "Hello sir, I am Sean, could I get past and have a look at the patient please!"

Dave nodded and moved to one side as Sean edged past him towards the bed. "I wouldn't move him!" said Dave to Sean. "If you notice, he has some wires coming from his head that lead into that machine on the table over there."

Sean leaned forward and gently felt where the wires were coming from. "These are not actually attached to the head but I'm not sure why they are there in the first place. So until then I am reluctant to move them!"

"Weren't you told of the possible dangers to you being here?" asked Dave although very pleased to see him.

"Yes, I was told something like that, but he is one of ours and I'm sure that he would do the very same for me if I were in his position, don't you!" replied Sean with a wry smile on his face.

"Good man," replied Dave relieved that there was now a medical person present with him and now Bill would stand a much better chance of coming through all this.

Sean, then took his stethoscope out of his backpack, and placed it onto Bill's chest and began to listen. "We could have a problem here.

For some reason this person's heartbeat is slowing down at a considerable rate. The reason behind that at the moment is a complete mystery." It was then that Sean moved his attention from Bill to the machine. He carefully picked it up and had a good look all around it. After replacing it back onto the table, Sean reached into his coat pocket and took out a pair of tiny earphones. As Dave watched, Sean proceeded to plug the end of the earphones into the machine and then he placed the other end close to his ear. After listening for a short while, he took the earpiece from his ear and said to Dave, "I have no idea what the hell's going on here but in my opinion this machine is somehow managing to be able to control this patient's heartbeat."

"What exactly does that mean?" asked Dave looking confused by the last statement.

"Well, if I am right, then as this machine slows down and down. So does the patients heartbeat. If left unchecked, it in theory could cause the heart to stop beating and that would be the end I'm afraid!" replied Sean.

"Can"

However, before Dave can get out another word, the barge was rocked violently side to side by four small explosions! Within seconds of the explosions occurring, banging could be clearly heard on the side windows of the barge. Dave pulled back the curtains to see Tom's face looking back at him. "You must get off the barge now!" shouted Tom at the top of his voice. "The barge is starting to sink!"

As these words hit Dave and Sean's ears, water began to enter the cabin space and was now lapping all around their feet. "That bastard seems to have thought of everything. Quick, we have to get Bill out of here!" said Dave to Sean.

"I agree, but if we unplug that machine then he could die!" replied Sean, looking between Dave and his patient.

Dave looked along the aisle of the barge and could plainly see that time was not going to be on their side at this time.

"Right grab you pack then take a hold of his legs," said Dave moving towards the head of Bill.

Then with one arm hooked under Bill's right shoulder, Dave's left hand took a hold of the headpiece and ripped it off Bill's head. Dave then shouted to Sean, "Go!"

The two men then picked up Bill, and began to wade through the water that by now was up to their knees. At the hatchway, many hands were there to reach in and grab a hold of all three men, dragging them all out of the cabin and finally onto the towpath. Sean took out his stethoscope and quickly listened to Bill's heartbeat. At first, it was very faint and the prognosis was not looking good. Then within a couple of minutes, new life seemed to appear and his heart rate steadily began to increase. When the others found this out they all cheered aloud like kids out on the playground. Bill, was quickly placed on a trolley from one of the ambulances and transported with a police escort to the hospital. Already waiting there for him was an armed guard that would remain outside his room until he recovered. Dave then placed a call through to Bill's wife up in Bolton. He then had the privilege to be able to tell her that they had managed to locate Bill for her and their son. Although he was on his way to hospital, the paramedic's prognosis was that he hoped that he should make a complete recovery. Through the tears, Rosalynd thanked Dave and the others for finding him and for bringing him home to them safely.

27

At the hospital, Dave waited with the other members of the team for the doctor's opinion after he had had a chance to examine Bill. Although the time dragged as they waited. Elation was prevalent now that they had managed to achieve what many strongly believed was impossible. Then the waiting was over when the doctor arrived to inform them that although he had not yet regained consciousness yet, his prognosis was that he would eventually make a full recovery.

With that information in mind, the members of the team all headed back to the Yard while Dave remained behind. "Could I go in and sit with him for a while?" asked Dave to the doctor.

"By all means but remember, he will not be able to hear you yet!" replied the doctor smiling.

With that, Dave stood up and after nodding to the armed guard who was standing outside the door. Dave quietly pushed the door open and saw his old friend Bill tucked up in bed surrounded by crisp white sheeting. To the side of his bed there were various drips attached to him. On the other side of the bed there was a heart monitor beeping away. Dave turned and looked towards the nurse who was present in the room and said, "Well at least his heart sounds a lot stronger than the last time I heard it!"

The nurse did not reply but gave Dave a reassuring nod of the head. Within a couple of hours, Bill's wife and son arrived at the hospital, after being met at the train station by Tom in a patrol car. Dave quickly brought her up to date with what he knew and then left then there in the room with Bill. A WPC remained outside the room to assist Rosalynd if she should need anything.

With the knowledge that Bill along with his family was now safe Dave hoped to be able to glean some further information from the now submerged barge. He had arranged that a team of police divers, be sent into the barge at first light, with the hope that they are able to salvage something that will enable the doctors to treat Bill successfully.

Dave wondered what significance the box had in this case and in what way it had affected, Bill!

The following morning the divers did make their dive into the barge and managed to retrieve several items of interest. One of the items found was DI Spears now knackered mobile phone. There were some syringes, along with an unknown substance, that they had discovered in the fridge. Those items were quickly passed onto the forensic chaps for their evaluation. They also discovered what looks like a delayed timing device that had been attached to the cabin doorway. This must have been triggered when entry was made and the timer was to allow time for the person to get right inside before setting off the detonators. The last thing retrieved was the box with the wires coming out of it that had been somehow attached to Bill's head while he had been lying on the bed. Once again it was going to be down to the techno chaps to try to discover the boxes little secrets.

The forensic tests on the substance found in the fridge, were quickly identified as coming from something that has been commonly used by men as a date rape drug. This must have been how Ferris was able to overpower Bill and be able to get him to the barge without too much fuss. How he then managed to keep him there is still a mystery. The one thing though was for sure, and that was that he must have had to keep Bill sedated throughout his ordeal otherwise Bill would have easily torn him apart!

Then Dave received a call from the techno boys, with regards to the tests on the black box. Their précis told him that there were actually no moving parts inside the box. There was however, plenty of electrical components that they had never seen before and this worried them. To Dave though, he knew that Ferris had previously worked for the government on top-secret things along these very same lines. He was convinced that the real answers to these questions would never see the light of day.

"If you had to make a stab in the dark as to what the box had been used for, what would it be?" asked Dave, interested as to what they would think it had been used for.

"A stab in the dark, you say. Well the consensus of opinion amongst us down here, is that it was some sort of pulse generator. Somehow, it was able to produce electric pulses that were then transmitted into the brain via the wires. What purpose they were for is unfortunately going to have to remain a mystery!" said Billy.

28

It was two days later before Bill was deemed fit enough to have any visitors, apart from his family that is. Dave found himself standing outside the door that lead to where his friend was. After all that had happened over the past few days, Dave was more nervous entering the room than he had been chasing down the killer!

Then before he could think, the door suddenly opened up and there was little Sammy standing there. Dave's eyes moved upwards from Sammy towards the bed where he had last seen his friend Bill, lying totally motionless.

"Well, are you coming in or not?" said a familiar voice.

It was Bill, and he was now sitting up in bed eating. Dave at first was unable to either speak or move and once more, the emotions began to well up inside him. Moving straight across the room towards Bill, Dave held out his hand and Bill took it. He then pulled Dave towards him and they embraced tightly as only old friends can.

"Well you look a dam sight better than the last time I saw you!" said Dave walking over and hugging Roz, Bill's wife. "Are you able to tell me what was going on with you all the time you were on that barge?"

"Oh, that's where I was," said Bill looking slightly bemused. Then he began to relay to Dave and Roz his bizarre story about the cold and hills and of course the part about the wolves.

Both Dave and Roz listened intently to Bills story and at times, a tear of two could be seen rolling down both of their faces as he recalled his nightmarish ordeal. When he had finished telling his story, Dave then filled him in on what they had discovered and who in fact had done this to him.

"Well at least he's dead now," said Bill looking relieved at that thought. "Because if he wasn't, then this sort of thing could have happened all over again and I might not have had you Dave, still around to save me!"

That last statement from Bill both pleased and at the same time embarrassed Dave.

It was while all of this was going on; all of a sudden, Roz gave out a loud laugh.

"And what may I ask is so funny?" said Bill teasing her.

"It has just dawned on me, why it was that you had those awful nightmares!" said Roz smiling. "If you remember, you hate the countryside and the cold and the reason that we cannot have a dog for Sammy to play with is because you heard that they all originally come from being wolves!"

This realisation brought laughter from everyone that was in the room. "So that box must have taken your fears and dislikes and then turned them into a living nightmare!" said Dave smiling that it was now all over. "Now that is scary!"

29

Two weeks later, Bill returned fully fit to work at Scotland Yard to a rapturous reception from everyone in the office.

No sooner had the frivolities ended, when Bill was summoned up to the Chief Constables office. Bill reappeared thirty minutes later with a beaming smile on his face.

"Well?" said Dave eagerly wanting to find out what had happened up there. "What did he want you for?"

"Erm, I am being transferred away from the Yard, to, would you believe it to your old neck of the woods, the Isle of Wight!" said Bill half-smiling. "And here's me not liking the countryside one little bit! So it looks like you will be getting another partner soon as well, Dave."

Dave was the first person to go and shake his hand and was genuinely pleased for his old friend. Bill had finally, been recognised for his experience as a police officer in his own right!

"Now all you have to do is to go and tell Roz the good news!" said Dave smiling.

THE END

Made in the USA
Columbia, SC
19 February 2018